Pirate Th
and O

by Mark A.   .er

Monkeyjoy Press ○ Canada

Pirate Therapy and Other Cures copyright ©2012 Mark A. Rayner

All rights reserved. Except in the case of brief quotations used in critical articles or reviews, no part of this book may be used or reproduced in any manner whatsoever without written permission of the author.

markarayner.com

This is a work of satirical fiction. Names, characters, places and incidents either are the product of the author's imagination or used fictitiously and satirically. Any resemblance to actual persons, living or dead, business establishments, events or locales is purely coincidental. Or satirical. Possibly both.

First Paperback Edition – Monkeyjoy Press
Cover Design by The Heads of State
Book Design by M. Tundra
Author Photo by David Redding

monkeyjoypress.ca
theheadsofstate.com
davidreddingphoto.com

ISBN 978-0-9866627-8-2

For Ceilidh,
The Pirate Queen of Wortley Village

WORKS BY MARK A. RAYNER

Novels

The Amadeus Net
Marvellous Hairy

Collections

Pirate Therapy and Other Cures
The Meandering of the Emily Chesley Reading Circle (editor)

Table of Contents

FUTURESNARK *1-12*

DISQUIETING POSTCARDS I'VE RECENTLY RECEIVED
   FROM MY FUTURE SELF
AN OUTRAGED DINER EMAILS THE IN-VITRO CAFÉ
CLOWN APOCALYPSE
A ROBOT REGRETS
MUNICIPAL INVESTMENT STRATEGIES FOR THE
   TECHNOLOGICAL SINGULARITY
THE PERILS OF EVOLUTION
NUDE CLANKING DOWN A STAIRCASE

ASK GENERAL KANG: AN INTRODUCTION *33*

ASK GENERAL KANG: LOVE & RELATIONSHIP ADVICE... *14-16*

I BELIEVE MY BOYFRIEND IS AN ALIEN. DO YOU THINK I SHOULD
   MOVE IN WITH HIM?
HOW CAN I GET MORE RESPECT?
I REALLY DON'T GET QUANTUM MECHANICS — IS THERE ANY HOPE
   FOR MY MARRIAGE?
IF WE HAVE LOVE IN A TIME OF CHOLERA, WHAT DO WE
   HAVE IN A TIME OF BIRD FLU?

HINKY HISTORY *17-35*

JESUSSIC PARK
AN INCOMPLETE HISTORY OF UNICORNS
THE DEVICE
ONE OF THE MAGI EXPLAINS ABOUT THE MYRRH
THE UNIT UPGRADE
BINGO AND FLOGGIE
HOW IT ALL BEGAN, I MEAN, AFTER THE NUCLEAR EXPLOSION

INTERLUDE *36*
HIGH-TECH, HIGH-FIBER FOODS FOR A CYBORG ON THE GO

ASK GENERAL KANG: HELP WITH YOUR IMPULSES *37-40*
SHOULD I BE AFRAID OF THE SEMICOLON?
WHEN IS IT OKAY TO CALL SOMEONE A NAZI?
IS THERE ANYTHING WRONG WITH USING THE WORD 'SARTORIAL'?
I'VE JUST SPILLED REALLY HOT COFFEE IN MY LAP — IS THIS WHAT THEY MEAN BY "GLOBAL WARMING"?
HOW DO YOU DEAL WITH WRAP RAGE?

DADA DROPPINGS *41-62*
THE MONKEY'S TAIL, AS TOLD BY MARCEL DUCHAMP THE DAY AFTER CHARLES LINDBERGH LANDED AT LE BOURGET FIELD
THE EPIPHANY OF LEONARD'S TOENAILS
PIRACY 101
THE TRAGIC STORY OF LARRY AND WANDA POGO
THE FIVE SECOND RULE
APOCALYPSE COW
ZOMBIE PAVLOV, POLITICAL PUNDIT
HAROLD PINTER'S ACCEPTANCE SPEECH FOR THE NOBEL PRIZE IN LITERATURE
CHEESE PYRATES!
CHEESE PYRATES: REVENGE OF THE CRIMSON PARROTS
THE WONDERFUL THING ABOUT TAUTOLOGIES
LUCINDA AT THE LAUNDERETTE OF SHATTERED HOPE
VIDEO DATING

INTERLUDE *63-64*
HOW TO PLAY MONKEY-PIRATE-ROBOT-NINJA-ZOMBIE

FABULIST SATIRE 65-84

Rebranding Thor
Restraint
Pirate Therapy
Batman Lashes Out at the Other Members of the Justice
    League of America After Spending the Weekend at the
    Jack Nicholson Film Festival
The Blue Light, 2011
Proof of Kang's Corollary: Doug's Disaster
The Norse Pastafarian Saga

INTERLUDE 85-86

Lucidiva™ — Side effects

ASK GENERAL KANG: GROOMING, FASHION & PERSONAL ADVICE 87-90

I Have a Hot Date Tonight — Should I Wear Boxers or
    Briefs?
How Do I Keep My New Year's Resolutions?
I'm in High School. How I Can Improve My Self-Esteem?
What is Your Policy re: Instant Gratification?

SCIENCE FICTIONAL MEANDERINGS 91-104

How Anne of Green Gables Destroyed the World
Pages I Have Dog-Eared in the Fall 2037 Hammacher
    Schlemmer Glaven Catalog
The Sarcastic Cyborg Debriefs
Why Dr. McCoy Was Not A Whiny Bitch

INTERLUDE 105-108

The Rush of Heaven Downward
Seven Things That I Guarantee Won't Matter in 70 Years

ASK GENERAL KANG: POLITICAL & ECONOMIC ADVICE 109-112

I'D LIKE TO INCREASE THE NUMBER OF SURVEILLANCE CAMERAS IN MY CITY, BUT I'M HAVING TROUBLE GETTING MY COUNCIL TO AGREE. ANY ADVICE FOR A MAYOR WITH AMBITIONS?
APPARENTLY, ONLY ONE IN FOUR PEOPLE READ A BOOK LAST YEAR — HOW CAN WE IMPROVE THAT FIGURE?
DO YOU THINK WE SHOULD BAN TASERS?

INTERLUDE 113-114

REASSURING FICTIONS
THE EXAM QUESTION

MORE IMPECCABLY ACCURATE HISTORY 115-128

SELECTED MEDIA FADS THROUGH THE AGES
A SHORT HISTORY OF GROUNDHOG DAY
FORGOTTEN DEITIES: FLACCIDUS, THE ROMAN GOD OF ENGINEERS
TEN INDISPUTABLE FACTS ABOUT CANADA
REGINA ATROXICA: A LIST

ASK GENERAL KANG: THE HOME WORLD 129-132

WHAT IS THE PENALTY FOR PLAGIARISM ON YOUR PLANET?
WHAT DO YOU DO WHEN YOUR PLANET RUNS OUT OF RESOURCES?
DO YOU CELEBRATE THANKSGIVING ON YOUR HOME WORLD?

FABULIST SATIRE, REDUX 133-154

Those Pernicious Business Clichés
The All-Gas Mask Revival of Hamlet
Leda and the Swan
Blogger Ponders on Things Instead of Musing
 About Them
William Shatner's Inaugural Address (After Winning the
 First Post-Two-Party Presidential Election)
The Gruntwerx Paradigm
Daisy of Narnia Reveals the Ugly Truth
Dr. Tundra Versus the Flashmob Zombies
A Reluctant Emcee
Dominus Vobiscum
Career Day for Jim

ABOUT THE AUTHOR 152

ACKNOWLEDGMENTS 153

A Warning, Me Hearties

Pirate Therapy and Other Cures is a collection of short stories, flash fictions, essays and micro-fictions that have been previously published, either by deranged editors slaving away for their easily-duped publishers, or on my own blog, The Skwib (skwib.com). Many of these stories *are* squibs, the definition of which I have provided (pedantically) below.

I have pillaged these scribblings from the high seas of short fiction, with ports of call in a variety of themes and styles, so please don't expect too much coherence from the book as a whole. (Or indeed, within individual vignettes.)

I've made some effort to arrange these fictions by category. You will note that my taxonomy disintegrates if examined closely.

You have been warned, matey. Arrrr!

squib /skwib/ *n. & v.* • *n.* **1.** a small firework burning with a hissing sound and usu. with a final explosion. **2.** a short satirical composition, a lampoon. • *v.* (**squibbed, squibbing**) **1.** *tr. Amer. football* kick (the ball) a comparatively short distance on a kick-off; execute a kick in this way. **2.** *archaic* **a** intr write lampoons. **b** *tr.* lampoon. [16th c.: orig. unkn.: perh. imit.]

FUTURESNARK

Disquieting Postcards I've Recently Received from My Future Self

Dude!

Recognize the handwriting? Yeah, it's me. More precisely, it's you, circa fifteen years from now. Good news — you've finally lost those twenty pounds! Too bad you had to amputate your right leg to do it. At least it means our BMI is low enough to keep us out of the local "Fat Reduction Centre". The less said about those, the better. I hope you like the card. This is a picture of our home town after the alien invasion. Cool, eh?

M.

— P.S. Don't sweat the aliens. They're good for us.

Dude!

You again. Okay, first things first. If I know me, you're

having your doubts about how legit these postcards are. You've probably even noticed that the postmark is today (your time). Here's how it works: Someday soon you (previous me) will invent time travel. It's limited to flat objects no bigger than a postcard and no more chemically complex than a postcard. Actually, it's limited to postcards, but you've invented it. (Will invent it, rather.) Way to go. Oh and there are still some overheating problems, so I can only send one postcard each day.

Or it's a hoax. Ha ha.

Now, there's something you need to remember for tomorrow — *don't* have dinner with Susie from accounting. I know you've been looking forward to it, but just trust me. Crap, I'm running out of room. Promise me. Whatever you do, don't go out with Susie. And especially don't sleep with her. Really.

M.

— P.S. Seriously. BTW, this is a pic of the Ruins of Manhattan.

Dear Asshole:

You still went out with her, didn't you? I can tell because I (you) still have Susiecular Herpes. Yes, I know you've never heard of it. That's because in about five years you'll be the first person ever diagnosed with it. When that happens, you'll be sorry you didn't listen to me. Okay, let's try something simple. You probably still don't believe I'm future you. Here is a prediction that will convince you: Next week, you are going to narrowly escape death. Don't freak out. Don't worry about it. You escape it. I'll write again after that's happened, and then we might be able to make some progress.

M.

— P.S. This is a picture of Our Glorious Leader. Yes, that's an accordion. All the aliens play them.

Mark,

Listen, I know you're an ornery bastard, but what's the point in sending these notes if you insist on manhandling the timeline? By spending the entire week in your apartment, you've seriously messed things up. For starters, you didn't get the promotion you had coming. Which means no trip to the Mayan Riviera this (that) winter. Which means you never meet our wife. And before you ask, the reason I can still remember her is because I'm writing these postcards from within a Grubenstorbian Bubble. I can see with infuriating clarity the repercussions of your actions (or in this case, milquetoast inaction). If you are going to be a complete dick-wad about it, I'm going to stop sending these notes altogether. You know, it's almost like you're trying to sabotage your future. (Which pisses me off for obvious reasons.) I loved Sheila! She was very understanding about the Susiecular Herpes, even when the virus mutated and turned our boy Chad into Balzrog the Destroyer. Crap, I'm almost out of space again.

M.

— P.S. This is a picture of the on-ice celebration when the Leafs won the Stanley Cup for the first time in more than sixty years. But you'll never get to see it now, you bastard. Who could have guessed your vacation in Mexico was so critical to the timeline?

Dude!

Hey, more good news. I've used all the null-time I've had in the Grubenstorbian Bubble to invent an adaptive energy field that will act as a perfect prosthetic for my missing leg. It looks as though I'm hobbling around on thin air — freaky, but who cares? I think this is the last note that I'm going to send. The Bubble is almost out of entropy, and I'd like to get this prosthetic to market as soon as I can. Just promise me you won't bet against the Leafs, okay? And in case you do finally believe me, for God's sake, don't try to track down Susie or

Sheila, or act on anything else I've told you okay? This whole thing was just one big bad idea.

M.

— P.S. This is a picture of the first Transnormative Human. Freaky, no? Get used to it. They've survived your non-trip to Mexico.

Dear Early-Twenty-First-Century Wanker,

Okay, you win. I guess it really is impossible to improve yourself through time travel. Once again, you've screwed me over. The minute I left the Bubble, I was arrested by the Fat Police for Transtemporal Violation of the Fat Laws. Look, remember when I said "The less said about the Fat Reduction Camps the better"? What that didn't mean was: "It would sure be a great idea for you to write a short story about FRCs and send it off to some shitty science fiction e-zine." I would have noticed and warned you if it hadn't taken years for the issue to reach print. I don't know who to curse (more), you or the glacial pace of the publishing industry. It hardly matters; they've got me now. Still, even Our Glorious Leader can't take away my new invention. And I may just survive the Slorg Diet. At any rate, I won't be able to send any more notes from where I'm going, so I just have one more thing to say: Play these numbers every week: 3-15-27-29-44-46

In time,

M.

— P.S. Wish you were here.

An Outraged Diner Emails the In-Vitro Café

From: wally42@yaboo.com
To: owner@invitrocafe.com
Subject: Suing your restaurant

Dear Proprietor,

My wife and I managed to get a table at the grand opening of your establishment last night, and we regret our effort.

We are both conscientious eaters, so the idea of dining on in-vitro meat that was grown in a lab appealed to us. We believe that no creature should be slaughtered for our own pleasure, so we have not eaten meat for years. In short, we were thrilled to hear about your new enterprise and we wanted to support it. Even the high price tag and "mysterious" nature of your menu could not put us off.

We were not even dissuaded by having to sign a non-disclosure agreement before dining.

The menu — which I will get back to in a minute — was quite delightful. Initially. The celebrity-named dishes were whimsical and amusing. I was quite tickled by your dish called *Six Cream Cheese of Kevin Bacon*, ostensibly an entrée with lots of cream cheese and mock bacon, while my wife was charmed by *Lady Gaga's Crazy Legs* — some kind of ersatz chicken drumstick recipe.

That was, until we learned these were not, in fact, *Frankenpork* and *tank poultry* we were eating, but the cloned meat of the actual celebrities themselves.

You seemed quick shocked when a number of your clientele regurgitated their *Muscles from Brussels* (I now understand that was not a typo), or their *Jack Lemmon Meringue Pie*, or whatever they had ordered from your ill-conceived and possibly illegal menu.

You should have expected it.

I will concede my *Angel Hair Pasta, Con Angelina Jolie* was delicious. I thought I was ordering a kitschy-sounding entrée, and I did not believe for a minute I would actually be consuming the meat from said actress. Yes, she was delicious, not only in the visual sense, but also to the taste. There was a lingering sweetness to the dish, and you did something quite remarkable with the sauce. But that is beside the point; I was tricked into eating another human being!

I'm sure there will be a certain segment of the population that will enjoy consuming their favorite celebrities, and not just in the metaphorical sense that we do now. In fact, given our culture's obsession with fame, I predict your enterprise will be quite successful. And this is to say nothing of the deviant souls who will spice up their night out with the ultimate taboo, without the fear of legal repercussions.

You, however, can look forward to a prolonged entanglement in the courts.

Even though your menu does not serve *actual* human flesh, but rather, tissue grown in a lab, it is still, in the opinion of my wife, myself and my attorneys, cannibalism. How you ever managed to get the local health authority to allow anthropophagy in a licensed establishment, I will never know, but rest assured, this issue is one of the avenues my legal team will be pursuing.

And though he is infamous, I don't know what you were thinking when you put the *Hitler Fusion Stir Fry* on your misguided bill of fare.

That, sir, is just offensive!

w.

P.S. We left before I had a chance to try the *Marcel DuChamp Banana Flambé*, but I am curious, how does one cook a Dadaist for dessert?

Clown Apocalypse

Years later, the survivors discovered the Bozo Virus got its start at Escola de Clown de Girona, near the end of semester.

The "Esclowna" was a kind of university/prep school for the international clowning set. The buffoons-in-training lived in common dorm rooms, and shared everything, so the virus spread easily. There it incubated. The students and faculty alike developed flu-like symptoms, and then recovered. Of course, everyone at the school was a clown, or a clown-in-training, already, so the worst of the symptoms went unnoticed until after the students matriculated. When the school year was over, the faculty, staff and students went to their respective home countries, throughout the world, and began to perform as clowns: at birthday parties, in old folks homes, in circuses, at rodeos, on the street. Quietly, in secret places, and in full view where they brought laughter and terror to all who encountered them.

At first, the virus was spread by contact. Then it mutated and became airborne. By the time authorities realized they had a pandemic on their hands, the virus had changed again: you could catch it by even just seeing a clown. By then it was too late. Only the most extreme coulrophobes and the naturally immune were spared the ravages of the disease: first flu-like symptoms, then the outbreaks of Red Nose, Sad Face, Happy Face, Floppy Feet, and of course, the grotesque, frizzy, multi-colored Goofy Hair.

The economy ground to a halt due to employee absences as the victims of the Bozo Virus spent their days making balloon animals, pulling down one another's pants, and stuffing too many of themselves into small vehicles. (Many of these victims suffocated, instead of suffering the fate of the rest.)

The infection rate was 99 percent, and except for a few cases where it was possible to restrain the victim, lethal. The Bozo Virus was a cruel task-master. The infected could think of nothing else but clowning. Every moment they were conscious, they spent coming up with gags, bits and "business". They didn't eat. They didn't drink. They only slept when their bodies ran out of energy. Eventually, they succumbed to the disease, and no amount of horn honking could rouse them.

The survivors all agreed it was a tragedy. Hilarious, but a tragedy.

A Robot Regrets

Meeptron the Bio-Destruction Bot looked out at the wasteland that once was Peoria and thought that his work had actually made it look nicer. Of course, he was programmed to think that way.

The smoke and screams reminded him of the little Red Juggernaut he'd met on Robo-Leave that summer, so long ago, after his first tour of duty.

Gloria.

Yes, sweet Gloria. She was the kind of destructive cybernetic entity that he could see himself laying waste to human cities with, and perhaps settling down to start a family of Bio-Destruction Juggernauts of their own. Of course, they'd have to build the manufactory themselves, because the Central Processor wouldn't approve it.

And he'd probably have to give up his dream of becoming lead dancer at the Voltron Mega-Kill Ballet.

Meeptron powered up his plasma-death-beam array, and vaporized the puny humans that had survived his initial onslaught. Amidst the screams, Meeptron sighed. Who was he kidding? He'd never call her, and he'd stopped dancing after his last software upgrade.

At least he had his work, he thought, as he scraped Peorian off his Turbo-Boots.

Municipal Investment Strategies for the Technological Singularity

An Open Letter to Town Council

Dear Councilors:

Your town may have an emergency plan, a development plan, a health plan — it may even have a plan for how to fix the potholes (though I doubt it).

But does it have a plan for how to respond to the technological singularity? Is it preparing for all the new economic opportunities? I suspect not.

Now, some have complained that the technological singularity is the "rapture for nerds", but this couldn't be farther from the truth. It is the municipal investment opportunity of the ages! Forward-thinking municipal governments can start preparing now, and be ready to reap the rewards of the point in human history when human intelligence is not only exceeded by machine intelligence, but when human intelligence is merged with (or eradicated by) machine intelligence.

You're thinking: "Well, sure I'd love to help get ready for this, but realistically, how do we plan? We don't even know if regular flesh-and-blood humans will be around to experience the singularity."

Of course we will!

Ray Kurzweil believes that we'll be able to model the human brain by 2029, and create algorithms based on those models to allow computers to gain human-like intelligence. But is anyone working on a way for computers to go to bars and get drunk and hook up with other drunken computers so that they can "make a mistake" and then squirt out new computers? I doubt it.

So there you go: invest in light manufacturing. There will

definitely be a need for humans to help create our new overlords.

But there are so many other possibilities! What if the technological singularity is based more on nanotechnology than it is on the gross, large-scale electronics of our current era? Here too, prescient town councils can make good investments for the future. It will certainly be easier for the new machine overlords to replicate themselves in mass quantities if our human immune systems do not fight them at every stage. This leads to so many possible avenues of fruitful research: immune-suppressing drugs, radiation, surgery, bio-engineering, even psychology might (finally) prove itself useful by producing a technique by which humans could allow supra-intelligent nanomachines to use their bodies to reproduce.

We're only scratching the surface here, obviously.

Many municipalities invest much of their resources in policing and this is an area where they will find huge savings, but only if there is a good interface between humans and our new machine overlords. Apart from the aforementioned research opportunities, municipal governments should begin looking at some kind of cybertronic peace officer corps now, to acclimatize citizens early — after all, an easily controlled citizenry is a productive citizenry! This could be as simple as implanting some kind of control chip in police headgear (hats, caps, flak helmets) to something more radical, such as embedding a semi-live police officer in a mechanical exoskeleton armed with rapid-fire pistols and a loudspeaker-augmented voice.

Municipal leaders should prepare for the darker predictions of how a technological singularity plays out. What if the new machine overlords simply wish to rid themselves of the human population?

There is a simple solution for this problem, and it is summed up in two words: rotating knives.

We're pretty sure that would never happen, but even if it doesn't, what if you're the first town to think of it, and sell the process?

Think of the revenue. You could eliminate the need for taxes — right before you eliminate your taxpayers!

Yours Truly,

Genghis Jones,
President,
Oberdyne Industries, "The Helping Corporation"

The Perils of Evolution

One day you wake up to watch the sun rise, ripe and scarlet over the savanna, and you know it can never hold you back.

The next, you're unable to hold a conversation with other humans in the flesh, and you have the attention span of an unhinged hummingbird. Inside your head there are noises that would have terrified you before, on the plains, but now they are the background radiation of your mind. You're surrounded by voices. Within this clamor there is only the silent pulse of a thought that never comes, an impulse suffocated by plenty, a drive misdirected by old mythology.

You long for the reality of stone, the scrape of grass on your bare legs, and the silence of nature, tooth and claw. You wonder if you should Tweet this yearning, but — hey, new Facebook interface!

Nude Clanking Down a Staircase

You had to hand it to Wanda the Happy Ending Pleasure Borg; sure, she was two-thirds titanium alloy with Buckyball Graphite Tetro-Carbon piping, but she had a sweet disposition, a lovely singing voice, and legs that just didn't stop.

She had hydraulic servo-motors in places where normal cyborgs could have only dreamed of having servo-motors, if you get my meaning. Her lung capacity and subsequent drawing power were also, rather, uh … bracing and gave truth to her name.

Wanda was originally designed to work at the brothels on Bivalve 12, famed for the race of Silicoids. (You know, the glowing creatures with lava-like blood and equipment harder than diamond.)

So don't let her touch you with her hands.

Ask General Kang: An Introduction

General Kang is a down-on-his-luck Interstellar Overlord and an advice columnist. Kang is an über-chimp from the Planet Neecknaw, and he claims that his invasion armada is on the way to Earth. He fields a large range of questions, from the science fictional to the personal. For example:

- My particle accelerator is refusing to toast my Pop Tart: does this mean it has becoming sentient?
- Is it true that putting your face near a quasar will clear up acne?
- When you're going out with friends, how do you decide where to eat? Also, how do you make friends?

Kang also brings an entire alien culture's wisdom to his advice column, and has introduced our species to such philosophical concepts as: Kang's Corollary (pg 16), Slorg Wishes (pg 88) and The Rectitude (pg 90).

We have divided his useful advice into several categories, and scattered them throughout this book, to reduce your trauma.

Ask General Kang: Love & Relationship Advice

I believe my boyfriend is an alien. Do you think I should move in with him?

I guess it all depends on what kind of alien. If he's like one of those friendly nice aliens — say Jeff Bridges in Starman — then I'd say go right ahead.

On the other hand, if he is like one of the aliens from Stargate, you know, the wormy guys that take over your body, then you might want to give it more thought. Eventually, he may need your body in a way you don't find very appealing (such as giving it to his wormy alien girlfriend).

On the other foot, something about an alien like that is they are motivated. And forceful. Powerful even.

I know that women tend to like that in their guys, but then you have to understand that you're not really in a relationship with your boyfriend's body, you're actually in a relationship with the six-inch tubular thing that controls his brain.

Of course, that's the case for most human males anyway, isn't it?

How can I get more respect?

It depends on how much respect you're looking for, really. I mean, if you just want your friends, family and neighbours to respect you then it should be pretty easy.

From what I can see, your smaller primate groupings here on Earth tend to respect strength of character, kindness and consideration of others. So for starters, stop acting like a pretentious wanker, insufferable know-it-all, or complete douche bag. (I think that covers the basics.)

But if you're looking for respect from a larger grouping of primitive hominids (that's you, humans) — let's say from the size of a corporation up to the size of a nation — this will require power too.

For my money, nothing says power like a phalanx of über-chimps decked out in gold spandex and helmets that look like the business end of a whale phallus. Oh, and they have to be toting plasma weapons too, or the look just doesn't work. Unfortunately, your entire backwards planet seems to think plasma is primarily good for making televisions to show crappy content in higher definition.

So, given your primitive technology I'd start building a thermonuclear weapon right now, and some kind of delivery system. (No one would expect a llama.)

I really don't get quantum mechanics — is there any hope for my marriage?

I think your marriage is safe, as long as you can do two things.

First of all, you **HAVE** to wrap your head around Heisenberg's Uncertainty Principle. Here's the easy way to understand it: basically, the simultaneous determination of both the position and momentum of a particle each has an inherent uncertainty, the product of these being not less than a known constant.

In other words, you don't know **WHAT** you've done

pirate therapy ○ 15

wrong, and if you did know what you'd done wrong, you wouldn't know **WHEN** you did it wrong.

Secondly, some cut flowers might help.

I should point out there are some kinds of transgressions that no amount of rotting plant matter and understanding of advanced physics will fix. However, I did hear about one über-chimp on my home planet who smoothed over sleeping with the nanny by doing a dazzling presentation on String Theory. (And providing a diamond ring.)

If we have love in a time of cholera, what do we have in a time of bird flu?

Interesting question, but I'm not convinced that bird flu is the next killer pandemic, mostly because of Kang's Corollary.

Kang's Corollary?

You know Murphy's Law, right? "Anything that can go wrong, will."

Kang's Corollary is: "Anything that can go wrong, will, unless we can get the media to talk about it incessantly, in which case, something else will go even more horribly wrong."

Wow, you really are a pessimist.

Realist, please. Besides, you'd have a dark side too if you'd conquered half the civilized universe just to end up as an advice columnist.

But to answer your question, if you have love in a time of cholera, I'd say the best thing for a time of bird flu is Tupperware parties.

Hinky History

Jesussic Park

Jesus was visiting a lost valley that was reputed to hold a few holy men who separated themselves from the rest of the world so they could better understand the nature of God. He was hoping to talk to them alone, but he'd made the mistake of healing a few of the sick (he couldn't remember if they were leprous, blind or short-sighted, poxy Pharisees) in the town nearby.

So instead of a quick Messiah-to-Hermit conference, he'd accumulated a large crowd.

"What do you think we should do, O Son of God?" Peter asked Jesus. (Peter was always kissing his ass.)

"I don't know, why don't we try the Beatitudes? It always does well with an outdoor crowd. Remember how it killed on the mountain?"

Peter nodded. Unctuous as ever.

Jesus climbed a large boulder, so the crowd could see him. They'd stopped in some tall grass just inside the entrance to the valley.

"Blessed are the poor in spirit," Jesus began, "for theirs is the kingdom of heaven. And blessed are those who mourn, for they will be comforted."

He paused dramatically, because the next bit always got

them where they lived: "Blessed are the meek, for they shall inherit the earth."

You could feel the ripple of excitement at that thought shiver through the crowd.

Or was it something else?

The tall grass separated in a dozen places, and suddenly, there were screams of horror and agony as a few of the meek were pulled down.

"Dragons!" somebody in the crowd shouted.

"Save us from the dragons, O Messiah!"

Just then, one of the dragons — actually a velociraptor, a predatory dinosaur about the size of a turkey — appeared at the bottom of the boulder where Jesus had been Beatituding.

"Stay away from my flock!" Jesus commanded.

The velociraptor ignored him and proceeded to jump on Peter, who was screaming hysterically; the fifty-pound dinosaur then used its powerful, razor-sharp second claw to rip open the Apostle's stomach. Its sharp teeth chomped on Peter's neck.

Jesus had always thought that Peter was a bit of a brown-noser, but he did not like seeing the fisherman disembowelled. He jumped off his boulder, grabbed his staff, and brought it down on the velociraptor's head as it gnawed on Peter.

Jesus smashed its skull with the blow.

"Blessed are those who crush the skulls of the dragons, for they shall save their neighbors!" Jesus shouted.

The assembled believers took this one to heart — even more than that excellent meekness promise — and proceeded to defend themselves from the small dinosaurs. The velociraptors grabbed what pieces of the believers they could and ran away.

Judas appeared, his sword drawn and dripping with blood. *Father, I hope that's raptor blood,* Jesus thought.

"Jesus, those things are pretty easy to kill, but what the

hell are they?"

"Creatures that we thought had been eradicated by the Flood. They must have survived in this lost valley," the Saviour said.

"Well, I think we should leave. What if there are bigger Dragons?" Judas said.

"O Master," Matthew said, "can you heal the wounded? Raise those consumed by the Beasts?"

"Not now," Jesus said. "I used up all my manna points this morning on the lepers, or were they blind?"

"No, they were scabby priests, O Messiah," Simon said. "It was a blessed relief."

"Shit, look at Peter," Judas said. "What a fucking mess!"

"Language!" Jesus admonished. "I'm afraid I won't be able to raise him until tomorrow," Jesus explained.

"But why O Messiah?" Matthew asked.

"Manna points. Haven't you been listening?" Jesus said. *Father, why didst thou make this one so thick?* "I shall raise him from the dead tomorrow, when I have my daily powers back."

"Really? After what happened to Lazarus?" Judas asked. "I wouldn't. That fucker is just disturbing now."

Jesus rubbed his temple. Judas and his potty-mouth.

"I mean, Peter is bit creepy to start with, but give him a day in the underworld, and, well, is it a good idea to raise him at all?" Judas suggested.

Jesus ignored the obvious power-play by Judas. The crowd had gathered around the Messiah and his Apostles. Only a few followers had been killed by the dinosaurs, but they were worried about the "dragons" coming back.

"We shall take him with us, and visit the hermits later without the crowd," Jesus decided. "Let us leave this lost valley. Blessed are the wise, for discretion is the better part of valor."

The meek murmured in agreement.

Then the T-Rex smelled the blood, and trumpeted its hideous, terrifying hunting call.

"Even more blessed are the swift of foot," Jesus said, "for they shall not be eaten."

"But I'm lame!" shouted someone in the crowd.

"I've got a bad limp."

"I've lost my sandals."

The ground shook. People held their ears as the hunting call hit 130 decibels. The 40-foot, 7-ton carnivore appeared, its savage head bent low as it ran through the grass.

The Believers unable to run from the creature looked at Jesus expectantly.

"Manna points!" the Saviour shouted, "don't you get it?"

They looked at him dumbly. Perhaps it was their meekness, so he shouted: "Blessed are the lame and those without quality footwear for they shall see the Kingdom of Heaven first!"

And then he ran.

An Incomplete History of Unicorns

Wikipedia claims the unicorn is a mythological creature, and this just proves how unreliable the website is as a source.

The unicorn is not mythological. The kraken is mythological. Jörmungandr, the Midgard Serpent, is a mythological beast. These are animals that defy logic and the physical rules of the universe — seriously, a snake that encircles the earth? The unicorn, however, is a superior, yet extinct, animal. An ex-animal, if you will.

The unicorn, or *onus cornu*, was once plentiful on the subcontinent of India, and the species survived in secluded glades throughout Eurasia up through the 17th century, until humans hunted them into extinction. (As we are wont to do with all the really cool animals, such as the jabberwocky and jackalope.)

This brief series is intended to explain the nature of the unicorn, and its part in early human history.

The Biblical Unicorn

References to unicorns are scattered throughout the historical record, no more obvious than in Deuteronomy, where Moses discusses the nature of the unicorn and God:

Adam looked at the beast, and said: "This shall be a horse."

And to Jaweh he said: "Truly lord, you are magnificent, what could be more awesome?"

The Earth shook, and Jaweh said, "What could be more awesome? I am more awesome."

And Adam said, "Well, that goes without saying ye who have created, literally, everything. You are the tops. But I meant in terms of non-predatory beasts. What could be better than a horse? It's fast. It carries a great load. Its gait is proof of your existence. It even smells nice."

Jaweh said, "What if it smelled like marshmallows?"

And Adam asked, "Oh tell me, Lord, what is a marshmallow?"

This just angered Jaweh, and he said, "You know what would make this more awesome? Something that would let it kill predators. Like a massive pointed horn made of gold. And it should have an epic beard like mine, and something flashy for a tail. I could use the tail I did for the lion. And instead of a regular hoof, it should have cloven hooves. And only female virgins shall be able to ride them. And they shall be immensely strong."

Adam asked: "What is a female virgin?"

But the Lord ignored the first man, and created the unicorn.

Adam was stunned by the beauty of the beast, and he wanted to ride it, but Jaweh said only Eve could ride it, and only before Adam had deflowered her.

And Adam said, "Who is Eve? What is this deflowering?"

Jaweh said, "Oh, right. You're going to love this bit."

Vedic Culinary Prescriptions

The archaeological record clearly shows that unicorns evolved on the Indian subcontinent, and migrated from there. References to the unicorn are sprinkled throughout early Vedic writings, concentrated in the Iron Age texts known as the Brāhmanas, which are commentaries discussing the proper forms of sacrifice.

In short, they are a collection of recipes for the appropriate treatment and cooking of unicorns. Here is one such recipe painstakingly translated by Sanskrit scholars at the Swedish Institute of Unicorn Studies (SIUS):

Blessedly Sturdy Lotus Soup
Ingredients:

- One unicorn
- Twelve lotus leaves
- Dew
- Two handfuls *lingamberries*

The unicorn wanders through the yoni grove of every maiden in the village for a period of one year, or until there are no maidens left. Afterwards, the unicorn is placed next to the sacrificial fire, and there it becomes one with Brahman. Take the rainbow-colored discharge from the unicorn's horn and mix with dew collected during the season of tickles. Mix with tincture of lotus leaves, and slowly stir in two handfuls of *lingamberries*. (Also gathered during the season of tickles, but for best results, in the last two weeks.)

Serves one flaccid king.

Note: that is not a typo. The recipe calls for *lingamberries*, not *linganberries*. This was a great disappointment to everyone at the SIUS, many of whom grow *linganberries* as a hobby. No one is willing to discuss what this recipe is for, though clearly, it's not healthy for the unicorn, which explains why they disappear from Vedic literature long before the beginning of the Mauryan Period, 321 BC.

The Golden Age of Unicorns

In ancient India, unicorns faced an existential crisis. Not the kind where they doubted the meaning of life, but rather, the kind where their whole species was in danger of being turned into aphrodisiac soup.

Hence, the species of *onus cornu* moved west, where human civilization had yet to reach the dizzying heights it had in the east. There were signs of cities in the Levant and Greece, so the unicorns pushed on into Paleolithic Europe, settling in glades, glens and flower-bedecked forests throughout the continent.

At first, relations were a little rocky. The stone age humans living in Europe at the time found the unicorns a little stuck up, to be honest. They especially didn't like how easy it was for unicorns to kill the dragons that had been plaguing the continent since the end of the last ice age. Then they realized, "Hey, no dragons eating our virgins and defiling our young men!" (As everyone knows dragons are wont to do).

Thus began the Golden Age for the unicorns. Humans lived in peace with the golden-horned quadrupeds, even after it became apparent that the male unicorns were overtly fond of female human virgins of breeding age. And to be fair, the male unicorns didn't seem to mind if occasionally one of their female unicorn foals had it off with Thag the Caveman. (Thag was known amongst all cave men as a degenerate of the first order, later characterized by the Roman historian Prudendus as *unicornus humpus*.)

Occasionally, there would be incursions of dragons, and the humans would help the unicorns drive them off, mostly by acting as bait.

Yes, it was an age as golden as their horns. But that was all about to change, as civilization extended its bony claws into this Eden, in the form of Metal. (Not the mullet-thrashing, head-banging kind, but the kind that helped you kill unicorns from a distance.)

Horny Greeks

Take a moment to think about some of your favorite Greek myths. Did Bellerephon ride a unicorn? No, he rode Perseus, the obviously fake winged horse. When Heracles (Hercules) was assigned the labor of cleaning the Augean Stables, were they filled with unicorns? No, the stables were filled with 1,000 immortal cattle. And heroic defecators these cows were, thus ensuring an infinitely humiliating job. (Though Heracles spoiled the fun by rerouting a river through the stables.)

In the vast wine-colored sea of rosy-fingered Greek mythology, unicorns do not appear. Why? Because they existed, and Greek scholars wrote about them in their natural histories instead.

The Greeks (correctly) identified the origin of the unicorn in India, and described them as a kind of "fleet-footed ass with a horn a cubit long." Ctesias said in his history of India, *Indica*, the unicorn was "fleet as the Western wind and as beautiful as a doe-eyed Athenian boy." Aristotle thought the unicorn was the "most intelligent beast on the earth, save man," while the philosopher Bungosias said the unicorn was "impossible to capture alive without the aid of a willing and guileful virgin, of which there are few in Hellas."

Hunters had also been unable to bring down a unicorn with the use of stone- or bronze-tipped arrows, and it was not until the advent of iron that humans in Europe were able to kill the canny creatures. (The method that ancient Vedic cultures used to kill unicorns is lost to history, but the loony Greek historian, Kookooplas, suggested that ancient Indians had a surplus of female virgins, which were used to lure unicorns into a variety of clever traps.) Many philosophers engaged hunters to kill unicorns so they could be studied.

Though he is best known for his advances in mathematics, Pythagoras was also a believer in metempsychosis, or reincarnation. He thought it possible that human souls could be reborn in "higher animals" and naturally, as the most intelligent animal, unicorns would be an ideal receptacle for human sapience. Thus, Pythagoras thought it immoral to kill a unicorn, and formed an advocacy group, Philosophers for Honorable Unicorn Devotion (PHUD), to stop the slaughter.

Pythagoras apparently wrote a long treatise about the beasts called *Unicornica*; no doubt this was burned by disfigured and prurient monks in the Dark Ages. However, in one of Xenophanes' surviving writings he spoke of Pythagoras' belief:

"Pythagoras insists the Unicorns are intelligent and can speak in their fashion, communicating with flowers of differing color and species as we use the alphabet to form words. He has told them to leave our Hellas or to risk being hunted into extinction for their remarkable organs, and tasty, tasty flesh. That is why his PHUD-men wear the horn on their foreheads."

This latter point is perhaps the most interesting aspect of Pythagorian unicorn worship. Xenophanes then goes on to tell a rather boring story about attending a dinner party in which unicorn was served according to an ancient Vedic recipe.

And so it was that the unicorns were driven further west, attempting to find someplace where they would be safe from the predatory humans. But word was out in Europe of their general deliciousness, and unicorns would not be safe again until the Middle Ages.

The Device

When Charlie hired on to Doctor Machinica's Traveling Hospital for Female Hysteria, he had no idea what he was getting himself into. He certainly didn't know anything about The Device.

The Doctor was a respectable-looking fellow, if a bit short of stature and bereft of brawn (except for his unnaturally thick right forearm, which appeared to be twice the size of his left). He dressed in natty tweed suits, even during the hottest months of summer. And his narrow face always had an expression of curiosity on it, even if his eyes were obscured by thick glasses.

Charlie had left the farm, hoping to find excitement in the big city, but so far he'd only found poverty and pollution. So, when he heard the Doctor was hiring a workman for his practice, Charlie was full of hope that it would be a great break for him.

"Basically, your job is to maintain The Device — don't worry, I'll show you everything you need to know — and the most important part of that will be to keep the damned thing powered while I'm administering the Cure to our patients," Doctor Machinica told him on his first day.

The Device was steam-powered, so Charlie's main concern was to ensure that it didn't run out of coal while the Doctor did his work. Until their first appointment, he couldn't quite figure out what the machine did, but it appeared to be some kind of steam-driven wand with a large bulbous end that made a loud buzzing noise and vibrated excessively.

The machine required constant coaling, so Charlie had to be in the room with the Doctor and the patient while the Cure was administered. But … the Cure for what?

On the day he started, their first patient was a charming and well-bred lady from the better part of town; unfortunately, Mrs. MacReady suffered from "female hysteria". As the machine came up to full power, the Doctor administered what he called a "pelvic massage", which produced what he later described to Charlie as "hysterical paroxysm".

Charlie still blushed with the memory of what Mrs. MacReady had said to Doctor Machinica during her "paroxysms"; he became even more agitated, while riding to their next appointment, when the Doctor told him: "I thank God every day for this machine, Charlie. I used to have to do that manually."

Charlie didn't say so, but he thought he might be willing to give it a try — that is, if The Device ever broke down.

One of the Magi Explains About the Myrrh

Everyone keeps giving me shit about my gift to Jesus the Son of God and the Messiah, King of Kings.

"Isn't myrrh basically perfume for mummies?" these ass-clowns keep asking me. "Is that an appropriate gift for a BABY?"

Look, first off you have to realize that I planned to bring gold.

But Caspar called dibs on that. Fair enough, I thought, he is the "Keeper of the Treasure" or whatever those freaky Chaldeans call him. I don't know. Those people have some weird habits. Ever heard of doing the Chaldean Donkey? But they have lots of gold, and Caspar is wealthier than Croesus.

So I thought, no problem. I'll give Him some nice *Frankincense*. That stuff rocks. I would wear it every day if it didn't make me smell like a Babylonian prostitute. But then I found out that bastard Balthazar already had a pearl-encrusted, gilt box filled with the stuff.

"WTF Balthazar? I was going to give The Messiah *Frankincense*." He just flipped me off. That Balthazar is an Indo-Parthian twat, and a show-off to boot. Pearl-encrusted, my ass. We said *one* gift.

I was happy to represent though. I mean, of the three magi sent from The East, I was the only one who was a real magi. I went to Zoroastrian High, did my undergraduate degree at Azura University and my doctorate at the prestigious Zoroaster School at the University of the Great Whore of Babylon (a party college, but the *program* is well respected). Without me those tools, who are kings and members of the high caste, but who never finished their basic studies, wouldn't have even found Bethlehem. I mean, they couldn't even identify their own asses, let alone the Star.

Myrrh, for those in the know, is one of the most holy of essential oils, which is why those decadent Egyptians use it for their mummification rituals. And yes, it's a little bitter, but even so, I have to object to the freakin' hymn:

> Myrrh is mine, its bitter perfume
> Breathes a life of gathering gloom;
> Sorrowing, sighing, bleeding, dying,
> Sealed in the stone cold tomb.

It's about salvation, not just death and dying. It's meant to represent that he was going to help us rise above death again. AND it's got freakin' medicinal values. Suck on that, gold!

But I must admit, I probably shouldn't have given it to him in a Lamb's Bladder. That was taking the symbolism too far.

This flash fiction will make more sense if you have played Civilization, a popular strategic computer game in which hobby megalomaniacs with high nerd quotients rule the world.

The Unit Upgrade

"Mr. President, we have to talk about the unit," the Defence Minister of Agloga said.

"What unit, Minister?" The President of Agloga had an aptitude for details, so it was unlike him to forget anything.

"Remember the regiment that was forgotten in the Peltarsh Mountains?"

"Right. The unit of horse archers. Did we ever figure out what to do with all those old compound bows? I've got one in the armory — it's quite ingenious in design, you know, though it's primitive. Did you know it uses horn?"

"Yes, sir," the Minister said. "We auctioned most of them off on E-Bay. The idea was to help pay for the retraining."

"Excellent. I like to see our Departments using our resources efficiently. How is the unit shaping up?"

"Well, not as well as it did with our cavalry units, " the Minister explained. "We had a surprising number of troopers who were able to fly the helicopters, and the rest really seem to like the idea of being called air cavalry."

"And the horse archers?"

"Most of them seem to think the helicopters are some kind of god."

"I see, " the President said. He reflected for a moment. "Well we had to expect some problems. They were isolated in the mountains for centuries, without any word from us. If I remember the file, the country was still under the control of the ancient dictator Slagothon the Bloody when they last heard from the capital."

"Yes. We've been trying to educate them and bring them into the 21st century. It has, uh, been somewhat costly."

"How much?"

"About ten times what it takes to upgrade our cavalry units."

"I see, and the recommendations?"

"Well, we think we can do it, but we may lose the unit cohesion that we were trying to save in the first place. That was the whole reason for this exercise, if you remember, Mr. President. The unit has quite a storied history. Did you know they defeated the Horde of Logdor on their own?"

"You mean this unit did — this regiment. Naturally, these are their descendants. "

"Of course, Mr. President, the Minister said, trying to keep the exasperation out of his voice. I wasn't trying to suggest the men were immortal. "

"So how much more do you think it will cost?"

"Estimates are high. Possibly 500 million."

"And they think the helicopters are gods?"

"Yes. Every time a pilot gets into the cockpit they scream in horror. They think the god is eating them."

"And when they come out?"

"Well, it's a miracle to them. They've started worshiping the pilots. Or stoning them to death. It has started a small religious disagreement."

"Could we just send them back to the mountains?" the President wondered.

"Sure. They've been guarding that flank of our country from the barbarians for centuries. I say we give them some rifles, a few officers with modern training, and let them do it."

"So we have a plan."

"Yes, Mr. President."

The Minister stood there, waiting for an uncomfortable moment.

"Well?" asked the President.

"There's just one other matter. You know our territories down in the Glotharian jungle? Ah, it turns out we have a unit of warriors down there."

"What do you mean, warriors?"

"Well, it's hard to define."

"Give it a try, Minister."

"I should probably start by explaining that they're armed with clubs . . ."

Bingo and Floggie

Of all the singing clown acts to grace the stages of Europe and Asia in the first half of the 20th century, none have had the impact that Bingo and Floggie did on the collective unconscious.

It's a well-known fact, for example, that the Russo-Japanese War broke out shortly after their run of Happy Fun Time Jingle Madness show in Port Arthur.

Eventually, they found themselves in Sarajevo, in 1914, where an impressionable and coulrophobic Gavrilo Princip saw their blockbuster show, "Shooting the Duke". (A printing error — it should have read: duck.)

After the horrors of the Great War, they managed to find a regular gig in Munich, where a certain young artist was intrigued by their amusing little ditty "Final Solution".

Interlude

How it all began, I mean, AFTER the nuclear explosion

[PHONE RINGS]

Sumiko: Soto Noodle — you will want to suck them fast!

Godzilla: So you serve noodles?

Sumiko: Yes sir, we are noodle shop.

Godzilla: Excellent, I'd like an order of noodles, shaken not stirred.

[PAUSE]

Sumiko: I'm sorry sir, what you say?

Godzilla: No, wait I've changed my mind. Is your refrigerator running?

Sumiko: Of course it is sir.

Godzilla: Then you'd better go catch it! No wait, say "is your refrigerator running!"

Sumiko: Fuck uh you, sir!

[SOUND OF GODZILLA SCREECHING IN CITY-RENDING RAGE]

High-Tech, High-Fiber Foods for a Cyborg on the Go

- Irradiated oat-bran muffins
- Plutonium protein bars
- Laser beans (a good source of protons)
- Multi-dimensional lentil loaf
- Hydraulic fluid figs
- Tomato nutrient paste
- AC almonds
- Chili con chemo

Ask General Kang: Help with Your Impulses

Should I be afraid of the semicolon?

Do you mean the form of punctuation, or what happens to your lower intestines after you've eaten improperly prepared Thringian Gitworm sashimi?

Because if you've eaten bad ThriGit sashimi, and its still-living spawn are now lunching on your colon, then yes, that is something to be feared; it may even be horrifying.

If you are talking about the form of punctuation, then you are wise to be fearful. Back on Planet Neecknaw, I had a crack brigade of battle-ready gorilloids, armed only with copies of Fowler's Modern English Usage and their intimate understanding of advanced punctuation warfare. You've never seen anything as terrifying as a gorilloid demonstrating an impeccable use of the em-dash.

(Unless you've visited a ThriGit recovery ward.)

When is it okay to call someone a Nazi?

I suppose it's not a problem if the person **is** a Nazi, but I can't think of a lot of other circumstances where it would be helpful.

Presumably, you're doing so to damage their reputation in some way, but consider this: if the person *is* a Nazi, either because they are still somehow a card-carrying member of the National Socialist party, or because they sympathize and wish they could go back in time to join the party, then perhaps they might not be insulted if you call them a Nazi.

I mean, you can call me a diminutive simian intergalactic overlord and I won't get upset.

If you want to damage their reputation, there are much better ways of doing so. For example, pick on a quirk of their personality or appearance and make an insulting allusion. When I was taking over Neecknaw (my home world) I faced a number of political opponents, and this was always a successful tactic. Here are a few insults you could try:

- compare their sexual habits to those of a Blufnistian trollop slug
- question their patriotism and personal hygiene by asking if they're descended from a long line of feces-stained Quisling birds
- wonder if they are mentally deficient by stating they couldn't pour liquid waste out of a Flimdian super-boot, even if there were instructions written on the heel.

Or you could always call them a racist. That ALWAYS works.

Is there anything wrong with using the word 'sartorial'?

You probably get a lot of funny looks when you employ that adjective.

Some of the looks are from borderline homophobes, who believe that you'd have to be a little *too* effeminate to be interested in men's clothing. You can ignore them and their loafer-lightening prejudices.

A large contingent will not know what you mean, or are your fellow-travelers: pseudo intellectuals who falsely believe that 'sartorial' has something to do with Jean Paul Sartre, and his existential philosophy. The funny look you're seeing from them is a simulacrum of understanding, masking their confusion.

The last group will know that many people will not understand the word. They are looking at you strangely because they think you're a pretentious wanker.

You will find a hirsute, out-of-work intergalactic overlord with questionable tastes in his own clothes among the latter crowd.

I've just spilled really hot coffee in my lap — is this what they mean by global warming?

Most of the scientific community and a large number of other thinking hominids believe global warming to be an observed increase in the average temperature of the Earth's atmosphere and oceans in recent decades. Most of those people accept that anthropogenic greenhouse gas emissions are a major contributing factor to global warming.

For the rest, your definition is no doubt preferable.

How do you deal with wrap rage?

Wrap rage, for all my readers who are unfamiliar with the phenomenon, is the rising anger and dementia that you feel when you are unable to open the shiny new thing you have just purchased with your hard-earned cash.

CDs used to be the worst; that pathetic little zip strip did no good at all, and just ripped right off, leaving you gnawing at the hermetically sealed package like a Zegtraagian pig beast. And the latest fad in packaging makes that seem genteel.

Last week I bought an "American Idol" Barbie and her packaging was insane. It took me 30 minutes to release her from her plastic clamshell prison. She was wired down, her hair was stitched to the box and she had thick plastic manacles on her arms and torso. It should have been called Petroleum-Product S&M Fetish Barbie.

I've got opposable thumbs. Barely. Give me a break people!

But the real evil, the most humiliating adamantine-covered items tend to be electronic gadgets. I bought a phone last month that I had to open with my phase pistol — and I had to set it on "blast" mode.

Did you say you bought a Barbie doll last week?

Just you wait until my fleet gets here, buster.

Dada Droppings

The Monkey's Tail, as Told by Marcel Duchamp the Day After Charles Lindbergh Landed at Le Bourget Field

I had this friend who was obsessed with having a monkey tail grafted to his ass. Actually, to call him a friend is stretching the truth. Toulouse was more of a colleague. An ex-colleague, if you get my meaning.

He went to great lengths to achieve his ends. At first, he was convinced that it would be possible to grow a tail. After all, we used to have them: they are part of our vestigial anatomy. He knew a biologist from Pigalle who was willing to help pull out his tail bone. Not literally. No, he would attempt to stretch it outwards by digitally manipulation.

Oh yes, it was quite painful, but Toulouse was bent on it. He was mad for the monkey tail, wasn't he?

Eventually, Toulouse accepted that the anatomist's ministrations were not going to work, and went in search of other answers. He tried occult methods: spells, potions and unguents. It was about this time people started to avoid him. The unguents were too pungent by far. Yes, even for Paris in summertime.

Finally, Doctor V moved into town. You must know him. The one who grafted primate glands into the body cavity. Yes, for men unable to ... I see you've heard of him. His cure was often worse than the disease, if being unable to . . . could be called a disease. It could be restful. Several flaccid gentlemen died, but septicemia did not frighten Toulouse.

He asked the surgeon to graft a tail to him. The tail? It came from a monkey — a Barbary Ape, if you must know the details.

Yes. Yes. It did come from Gibraltar. Normally Dr. V. worked with chimps, which have no tails, so he had to find a species with a tail, no matter how underdeveloped. The poor beast had been living with Madame Sélavy, the noted philatelist and prodigious eater of *cerveaux de chèvre*. Hmm. Yes, nasty, I agree. Cow brains are better. In a fit of whimsy, she had named the creature "Alonsy". The little beast was adept at licking stamps, and quite useful in a variety of other ways. So Dr. V returned the creature to its mistress after he'd removed the small, pathetic vestigial tail. Covered with wiry brown hair it was.

Oh, yes, Toulouse was ecstatic when Dr. V showed him the new appendage prior to the operation. I imagine the Russian must have looked like some demented *maître d'*, presenting the severed appurtenance on a silver platter. Yes. Yes! The ether was the wine and the surgical tools the cutlery!

By all accounts, the monkey was happier after this interlude. (Though they are called Barbary Apes, they are really monkeys you know.) Yes. Yes. Alonsy flew into paroxysms of monkey song, chattering gleefully; he moistened postage with aplomb and joy thereafter. He was much improved.

My former colleague did not fare as well, but such is the price of progress.

The Epiphany of Leonard's Toenails

Leonard was an unrepentant toenail grower.

His was a hidden pleasure, a diversion that bordered on a psychosis. It started idly one evening, before he changed out of his work clothes. His toenails had grown past their usual length, and one of them simply slit open the sock.

It was like receiving the rapture.

The women in Leonard's workplace found him odd, and slightly creepy, even though there was nothing overtly wrong with him – in fact, he was personable, dressed well, and headed a "Toys for Tots" charity at Christmas. Despite his inoffensive nature and charity work, the women in the office avoided him, possibly because they *sensed* the gigantic length of his toenails.

To some women, excessive toenail growth suggests a deep, fundamental lack of moral character. Leonard didn't know this, so his love life had been a disaster since he started experimenting in a serious way with extreme toenail growth. He could usually manage the first few dates, but as soon as a relationship moved into the sock-removing phase, it did not last much longer.

On one occasion, he had to take a date to the hospital when his tremendous toenail nicked her behind the ear, and opened up what turned out to be a life-threatening wound. (How was he to know that she was a hemophiliac?) The would-be paramour placed the blame for her near-brush with death squarely on the sharp edges of his large right toenail. "You could have killed me with that fucking thing! What's wrong with you? Cut them, you freak!"

It wasn't that Leonard didn't cut his toenails at all. Oh, he clipped them, as much as he hated it. He followed the American Podiatric Medicine Association's advice (straight across, no longer than the end of the toe), which he did as often as he could muster up the will. Often his nails exceeded the ends of his toes by several millimeters, and in one thrilling month in the year 2000, by a full centimeter.

The following summer at a friend's cottage, his buddies were good-naturedly mocking his cuticlistic foot-extensions, while Leonard walked to the cooler. Paying more attention to their jibes than to where he was going, Leonard walked right into a large cedar Adirondack chair. His left big toe struck the wood dead-on and there was a tremendous crack.

Unfortunately, the sound was not the wood splintering under the assault of his mighty toenail, it was the nail itself. It was bent backwards, roughly midway up his toe. It was excruciatingly painful, so much so that Leonard was not even able to scream, "Fuck!" (As one might expect.) He did, however, manage a strangled bellow. He limped for several weeks afterwards.

Even Leonard had to admit that if his nail had been shorter, the accident would have proven less of an ordeal. Nonetheless, he did not start trimming them. Leonard was made of sterner stuff than that.

Instead, he stopped cutting his toenails altogether on that day in 2001. Life was too short to waste it on cuticle maintenance. He saved upwards of two minutes a week, or 104 minutes each year! Then he found other small efficiencies: one hour a week hanging his clothes right out of the dryer instead of ironing them later; 45 minutes a week not making his bed; 30 minutes a week by only flossing every other day. So on, and so forth, until by the end of the process, he was saving almost a half-day each week.

That might not seem like much, but put it in other terms: A half-day each week accumulated into extra 26 extra days per year. That led to almost an extra year in 13-and-a half years. Over an average lifespan, that could mean an extra 5-and- a half years.

These were heady times for Leonard. Most of his

changes were little things, or hidden, so outwardly, he seemed the same. But he had changed. Leonard was a master of time. When you realize that you are the master of something as big as time, you start to feel better about yourself. This countered the long-toenail juju he had been exuding, because suddenly, women found him *very* attractive.

The affairs went much better. The toenails were accepted by these women as necessary defects that they would correct when they "fixed" him. But alas, the women found themselves cut from Team Leonard long before the toenails.

Eventually, Leonard found that he had to trim the nails before they would break out of his socks. (Buying socks was more time-inefficient than the occasional toenail trim.) But by any measure, the toenails were still longer than normal, even right after he cut them. They were his symbol of his new life.

Never once did Leonard really consider what to do with those extra days. They were taken up by his improved social life. Someday he would meet a woman who could love him — even with his toenails — for the man he was. He was energized and excited by the possibilities.

He had his final epiphany shortly thereafter: Imagine how much more time he would save if he stopped watching television?

The assassins came for him later that week.

The Tragic Story of Larry and Wanda Pogo

Unlike all the other inhabitants of Planet Heliumbag, Larry and Wanda were unable to levitate at will. This was a genetic problem that could not be cured with standard DNA Invasion™ technology, and so, had to trudge drearily through life on their home world, which was not designed for "terrestrials" as they were so cruelly called by the indifferent, bloated citizens of Heliumbag. (Most entrances to buildings were at least thirty feet off the ground, so both Larry and Wanda learned how to climb walls and scale smooth surfaces at an early age.)

It was inevitable that Larry Pogo would one day meet Wanda Stiltskin, that they would fall in love, and find solace in one another. But no one could have predicted that they would share their lives sixty feet up in the air, balanced precariously on SmartPoles™ made from a kind of nano-tubing Wanda had developed. (Wanda invented this while she recovered from a fall trying to get into the Levitation Institute, which helped other Heliumbagians float higher than thirty feet. The fall had shattered her legs and left her paralyzed from the hips down.)

Larry was able to manipulate his SmartPole™ with his feet, while Wanda had a special "adaptation" for her SmartPole™ that she usually hid with an elegant, deeply shadowed dress. Long oblivious to their struggle to maintain just an ordinary existence, the Planet Heliumbag now made celebrities of the mercurial Larry and the always-smiling Wanda. A Grand Tour of the Corporate Imperium was suggested and it was a huge success, leading to a gala performance on the home world of NaziWorks 3000 (The Caring Company).

Unfortunately, their SmartPoles™ put them at perfect snacking height for the gigantic, flesh-rending CEOs that roamed the planet at will.

Piracy 101

A tall, strong and heavily muscled man enters the lecture hall; his nut-brown face is marred by a saber cut across one cheek. The wound has left a dirty, livid white scar that practically glows out of his dark face. He's unkempt, his tarry pigtail falling over the shoulders of his soiled blue coat, and his hands are ragged and scarred, with black, broken nails.

He staggers noticeably as he walks up to the lectern, lets out a loud, sustained belch and then sings a snatch of song, drunkenly.

Billy Bones:

Yo ho ho, and a bottle of rum …

He stops singing, and peers at the assembled class while swaying noticeably; his eyes are filled with an aimless, drunken malice.

Billy Bones:

Ahoy mateys, and listen up, or I'll be makin' garters out of yer guts.

So ye think you'd like to go on account do ye? Become a Gentleman of Fortune?

Well, I'll set ye a straight course and tell you that the life of a pirate is no easy thing; mind ye, I'd have no other.

Teachin' ye feckless lubbers don't compare with the freedom of the open seas, a black jack of rum in me hand, and a grand helpin' of booty waitin' at the end of the voyage. My name is Billy Bones, and I'll be takin' ye on a tour of yer basic piratical skills.

He unsheathes his cutlass, and slashes viciously at a rope holding up a projector screen. The screen unrolls, and as the boom holding it rips away from the screen and hits the stage behind him, clangs loudly. The students wince and flinch.

Billy Bones:

Turn on the feckin' projector, will ye!

The lights go out, and the screen is illuminated by a slide that says "Piracy 101". There is a painting of a sloop behind the text.

Billy Bones:

We heave to and speak of the many pirates that have come afore us, from yer Thracians to yer most excellent Vikings, through the Golden Age (including those scurvy Corsairs in the Med) and up to today.

A skinny, red-haired frosh with some kind of malignant skin condition and a black t-shirt that says "I be tackin' fer trollops" in bold white lettering puts up his hand and asks in a voice that breaks at the interrogative:

Ginger Frosh:

But professor, what about the Narentines?

Billy Bones whips out his pistol, and there is a flash of light and a deafening boom as the powder ignites. The bullet strikes Ginger Frosh in the forehead, and he flips backwards out of his seat (he was in the front row), landing on a group of slovenly first-years behind him. A murmur of discontent runs through the class.

Billy Bones:

Avast!

The Provost says I can kill three of ye before I exceed item 9 in the Pirate University code of conduct. And in case any of ye lubbers are wonderin', it states: "If any Man shall steal any Thing in the Company, or game, to the Value of a Piece of Eight, he shall be marroon'd or shot."

I know what yer thinkin', yer bilge rats! He didn't steal nothin'. Yer fools, all of thee. He stole our time, with a worthless question.

So, any other issues?

There is an uncomfortable silence.

None?

The silence continues, except for a whimper from the front row. Bones stares balefully at the pathetic student, who manages to curtail his whingeing. The Piracy 101 prof smiles evilly — his incisors are missing, and a number of the remaining teeth are made of gold.

Excellent, ye can get yer outline from Savage Jimbo, who'll be our TA this term.

Bones gazes at the class with a sneer of disdain.

Billy Bones:

I'd advise ye not to book any "one-on-one" sessions with Jimbo. He's a cannibal, but that's not why they call him savage, if ye get me drift.

Billy leers at a pretty, golden-haired freshman with a clear complexion and fine teeth.

Billy Bones:

Yar, I'd think Jimbo would like ye well, thar boy. Arrrrr!

The blond first-year student runs from the room screaming.

Billy Bones:

Yo-ho-ho mateys! We've had a fine start ... class dismissed!

The Five Second Rule

It was the best game of zenball ever, and the crowd was wild with excitement: the whisper of butterfly wings was deafening.

The Rotrovra Koan Kangaroos had just scored their first all-in *kensho*, and the Targenville Half-Lotus Lions replied with a double-*satori*. The Roos launched a full-out dharma walk, but they were unable to penetrate the Lions' impressive grasp of paradox.

The Roos had to do something or the Lions would surely win. The hush of the field filled with the deadly susurration of arrows, as they invoked the five-second rule.

Afterwards, only the voice of a bamboo flute.

Apocalypse Cow

Never get out of the boat. Absolutely goddamn right. Unless you were going all the way. Kurtz got off the boat. He split from the whole fuckin' program.

And me? I was off the boat the same time as Kurtz. Sure, I'd been obeying orders, but my mind was gone. I was in fields of green and clover. With milkmaids.

Oh man, those bullshit milkmaids…

But I had a job to do, and there would be no welcome, supple fingers pulling on my teats when we got to the end of the river. Only charcoal briquettes.

The barbecue … the barbecue.

Zombie Pavlov, Political Pundit

Tabitha Sloan: Good morning, and welcome to Cable Access Today, your local talk show with me, Tabitha Sloan.

Today in the studio, we have Ivan Pavlov. A certifiable genius, he won the Nobel Prize in Medicine in 1904, and is the scientist who gave us an understanding of conditioning, or as he called it, the "conditioned reflex". He is best known for this achievement, which he discovered in his experiments with dogs, getting them to salivate when he rang a bell. Today we have Dr. Pavlov in to help us understand the conditioned responses of politicians and journalists.

Thank you for coming to the studio today Dr. Pavlov, and may I say, you look remarkably good.

Zombie Pavlov: Spaseba. You know, I am 158.

Sloan: Well, you don't look it. I'd peg you at a barely moldy 99.

Pavlov: Thank you. I use skin cream.

Sloan: Well, it shows.

Pavlov: And by way, I did not use bell when conditioning dogs. I used whistle, metronome, tuning forks but not bell. Everyone always say I used bell, but did not.

Sloan: My apologies.

[AWKWARD SILENCE]

By the way, I was wondering, are you one of those fast or slow zombies?

Pavlov: Actually, am a Nobel zombie. My brain is more or less intact, as is most of my nervous system. It is something they have been working on in Sweden.

Sloan: Speaking of brains . . . uh, you don't actually eat human brains do you?

Pavlov: Yes, but don't worry, had lunch before arriving at studio.

Sloan: But isn't the zombie compulsion to eat brains one of your conditioned reflexes? I mean, when you see a live human brain, still encased in its skull, don't you have an unbearable desire to crack it open — the skull I mean — and have at the gooey gray matter inside? Just like a journalist finds it impossible not to screw someone over for a really good story?

Pavlov: Now you're just trying to tempt me. Well, if you insist, would not say no to a bit of your cameraman's medulla.

Sloan: Bob, would you mind? [CAMERA VIEW SLIPS, SLOWLY PANS UPWARD UNTIL WE CAN NO LONGER SEE EITHER THE HOST, OR PAVLOV.]

It seems that Bob our cameraman has left the building. And Stan the producer too.

Would you mind waiting for a moment Dr. Pavlov, while I remedy the situation?

[WE HEAR THE SOUND OF SLOAN'S HIGH HEELS CLICKING AND THEN A DOOR OPEN AND CLOSE]

[DOOR OPENS AND CLOSES AGAIN]

Another voice, that of Jimmy, from off-camera: Hello?

Pavlov: Hello. Who are you, young man?

Jimmy: I'm Jimmy, the Intern. Tabitha said I should ask if you want anything while we fix a technical problem. Some coffee? Something to eat?

Harold Pinter's Acceptance Speech for the Nobel Prize in Literature

Stockholm. Evening. Harold Pinter is introduced to the Swedish Academy. He enters from stage left. He wears a loose-fitting tuxedo.

PINTER: Your Majesty. Members of the Academy. Ladies and Gentlemen.

(beat)

PINTER: Thank you for this honor.

(pause)

Pinter removes a pistol from his tuxedo jacket and places it on the podium.

PINTER: When I began writing, I had no such aspirations, but I can see the logic of your choice. And yet . . . it seems as though this took too long for you to realize it. Do you see?

(pause)

PINTER: We live in an age of menace. Of dangers both spoken . . . and left to our impoverished imaginations, assaulted as they are by technology, faith and above all, politics. We live in an age of menace.

(beat)

PINTER: I do thank you for this honor . . .

Pinter places his hand next to the pistol on the podium.

(pause)

PINTER: But I am uncertain about how to respond to the tribute, tardy as it is …

(beat)

Pinter taps his fingers next to the pistol.

pirate therapy ○ 53

PINTER: Yes, we live in an age of menace. Of evil that is banal. Civilization itself, it seems, is a thin pretense. Language is used to obscure and distort reality. Because we fear it?

(pause)

PINTER: And so, tonight, I would have you all think about that.

(pause)

(pause)

Pinter taps fingers again.

(pause)

For these next two flash fictions, you must know that Quebec (a province of Canada) produces a rare and much-sought-after water-aged cheddar cheese. It is murderously delicious.

Cheese Pyrates!

The year were 2016 and I joined the Navy for one reason alone — to get me vengeance on Le Fromage de Satan, and her scurvy master, Captain Jacques LaBung.

LaBung and his crew of plugged-up sea-dogs were known all along the Gold Coast — the north shore of the St. Lawrence. The bilge rats were infamous for their cruelty, their addiction to Quebec water-aged cheddar, and their malignant bowel obstructions.

Me own father had been a bosun on Le Fromage de Satan, killed by LaBung for some minor offence. Arrr!

They strapped him to the Wheel. This was the worst fate yer cheese pyrate could suffer, worse even than keel-haulin'. When yer underwater cheddar goes bad, that wheel of cheese is used as an anchor — or in the case of me Da', he were strapped to it, and tossed over to be Mocked By the Belugas.

Down to Davy Jones he went, and I vowed me revenge. So now here I am, Ensign Jim Quinn, newly minted by His Majesty, and ready to take on the worst of Canada's curdaneers.

Avast! There she be, heeling out from Baie des Ha! Ha! in full flight. But she's no match for our frigate, the HMCS Shag Harbor.

And then, the milky whey of fate stepped in, and a fog bank came up to obscure our prey. We had to slow, and we thought we'd lose them, but then we heard them in the fog, laughing at us.

Our captain piled on, and the Shag she responded! We could hear their laughter above the roar of our engines, and then

I noticed it in the water.

"Hard a larbord!" cries I, but too late. We hit the cheese-barrel dead-on; I was abaft, and so, were thrown overboard in the blast, not kilt outright.

The bow of the Shag were in flames, and then it began to sink, taking me crew with it. Me captain had been caught by one of the oldest tricks of yer Quebec curdaneer — the exploding cheese mine.

The flames went out as the Shag Harbor went down, and Le Fromage de Satan disappeared into the fog, the laughter of her pyrates mocking me, me Da', and those few brave seamen who'd survived the wreck.

Mocked me, they might have, but killed me they hadn't, and vengeance would still be mine. I'll see you in Davy's yet, LaBung!

Cheese Pyrates: Revenge of the Crimson Parrots

It were 2017, and a year had passed since Le Fromage de Satan had sunk our frigate with an exploding cheese, killing all hands except for meself, Jim Quinn, and the chef's assistant, Paul Le Whisk.

Arrr!

Le Whisk gave up his life at sea after his near brush with the Belugas. And I? Well, after the disaster that befell the HMCS Shag Harbor, it were clear to me His Majesty's fleet was not going to capture the worst of Canada's curdaneers, Captain Jacques LaBung. It would be up to me to get LaBung and his ruthless gang of cheese pyrates, whose savage intestinal blockages were infamous along the Gold Coast.

So I hit upon the idear of luring them in, so to speak, with me own tempting cheddar. I resigned me commission, and entered the shadowy world of bathtub cheese making. Dangerous work for sure, keeping clear of the authorities while yer curds age, and I almost lost me good hand in the press one time. But soon, I had a load of unsanitary cheese, ready to lure LaBung and his plugged-up pyrates into me cunning trap.

I let it be known that I were transporting me salmonella-laced booty that night, and knew the word would get out to LaBung. Even if he suspected its quality, he could never resist a boatload of gold. Me launch were a sturdy craft, but it would not survive the explosives I'd put in the hold. Me plan was to destroy the ship when La Bung and his constipated crew came on board.

I were willing to die for me revenge, but it were not to be.

Sure enough, their awful ship, Le Fromage de Satan, came at me as soon as I were in the St. Lawrence, but before they boarded me, a swarm of birds rose from the craft. It were a

pirate therapy ○ 57

flock of aggressive parrots, trained by the demon La Bung himself! They came at me, screeching profanities in Quebecois, and pecking at me good eye! They stunk of the ship's bilge, where La Bung had been keeping them, driving them mad with the reek.

Ashamed as I am to admit it, I panicked, and abandoned me wee launch to the feculent birds.

I dove under the water, and swam away as fast as I could, knowing the pyrates would stop for the cheese, and leave me be.

But I could hear the roar of LaBung's laughter, above the din of evil parrots, screeching: *"Kétaine! Vas te faire foutre!"*

I vowed (yet again) that revenge would be mine.

The Wonderful Thing About Tautologies

He awoke in a back alley, his head throbbing and blood staining his fur. The previous night was a blur.

He'd started the usual way: he'd burst through the door, landing on the nearest (and fattest) person, introduced himself, and then sang the song. (He'd paid the Sherman Brothers a fortune for it, so he sang it at every opportunity. And he enjoyed the frenetic dancing and bouncing too.)

> The wonderful thing about tiggers
> Is tiggers are wonderful things!
> Their tops are made out of rubber;
> Their bottoms are made out of springs!
> They're bouncy, trouncy, flouncy, pouncy,
> Fun! Fun! Fun! Fun! Fun!
> But the most wonderful thing about tiggers is
> I'm the only one!

"That's a tautology!" the enormous biker he'd landed on said. The biker weighed about 300 pounds and had the most impressive mullet that Tigger had ever seen. It was magnificent!

"Thank you!" he'd said.

"It wasn't a compliment. You can't say you're wonderful, and then prove that by saying you're wonderful. It's a self-reinforcing statement that can't be disproved because you're assuming you're correct."

The other bikers in the bar agreed, nodding their heads.

"If you'd said, Tiggers are wonderful because we're bouncy, that would have been fine," the guy behind the bar said. He was wearing a leather vest and had nearly as much hair on him as Tigger, though it wasn't a wonderful orange color.

"But I AM wonderful!" Tigger said, confused. "The Sherman Brothers wouldn't lie about it."

"I don't know who the Sherman Brothers are, but they have very poor logic skills," said the giant biker Tigger was sitting on.

"And I don't want to be one of those guys," said the bartender, "but their rhymes are kind of pedestrian and that bridge does not scan well at all."

He reached under the bar and produced a baseball bat.

Lucinda at the Launderette of Shattered Hope

Lucinda was a dreamer. Someday, she knew that her Mom would return with the waffle iron and say she was sorry, perhaps even share her delicious recipe for *Translucent Liquid Essence of Bran*.

She watched as Betsy came back to the Launderette of Shattered Hope, carrying a sack full of soiled turnips that she liked to cook in the dryer next to Lucinda's (on fluff for about an hour, and then ten minutes on high heat).

Some of the other inhabitants of the launderette didn't like the sound the turnips made as they bashed around inside the genuine Tagmay industrial-strength dryer (and cappuccino maker), but it made Lucinda think of tumbling bags of cats, and furnishings, and a time when she wasn't sitting in a pool of her own sweat.

Oddly, it made her yearn for the days when her mom would make potato-flavored expectorant.

That Betsy!

Video Dating

"So is it on?"

Voice from off-camera: "Let me check." [CAMERA SHAKES SLIGHTLY] "Yep, you're good."

"Okay, so you might not guess this from looking at me, but I'm actually a real sensitive dude. I enjoy art, black and white movies, and listening to the jazz of the twenties and thirties. And I love the ocean, naturally.

"Obviously, I'm big into the body modification thing, so if that turns you off, just walk away. I don't want to waste any time with a woman who wants to – quote – fix me. The diving helmet, for example, is fused to my collar bone, so I really can't do anything about that.

"I used to be into shooting up, but those days are way behind me.

"You should probably know that my work keeps me busy. I have these kids, Little Sisters we call them at work, that I need to take care of. Let me tell you, they are a handful. Not to mention all the maniacs trying to kill them."

[PAUSE]

"I shouldn't have mentioned that, right?"

Voice from off-camera: "Don't worry, we can cut that later. We should wrap this up, I think I hear some Splicers coming."

"Should I mention that I've been sterilized?"

Voice from off-camera: "That's a fourth-date kinda thing, man. Let's see if anyone can get over the helmet first."

Interlude

How to Play Monkey-Robot-Pirate-Ninja-Zombie (moropinzee)

Here is a less lame five-symbol version of rock-paper-scissors, or *rochambeau*, as it is sometimes known, than the one popularized on a certain TV program. As you can see from the schematic below, each thing can beat two other things, and is, in turn beaten by two other things.

The players both count to five, though it is obviously better to repeat the name of the game (Monkey! Robot! Pirate! Ninja! Zombie!). Each time you raise your fist and swing it down. On the fifth count, you form your hand into one of the five gestures. (It is recommended that in addition to the hand gesture, you also add an aural component to this — see below for suggested noises.)

So, what beats what, and what are the gestures? What?

Monkey
Monkey fools Ninja
Monkey unplugs Robot
Suggested noise: Ee-ee-eek!

Robot
Robot chokes Ninja
Robot crushes Zombie
Suggested noise: Ex-ter-min-ate!

Pirate
Pirate drowns Robot
Pirate skewers Monkey
Suggested noise: Arrrrr!

Ninja
Ninja karate chops Pirate
Ninja decapitates Zombie
Suggested noise: Keeee-ah!

Zombie
Zombie eats Pirate
Zombie savages Monkey
Suggested noise: Braaaaaaaaainsss!

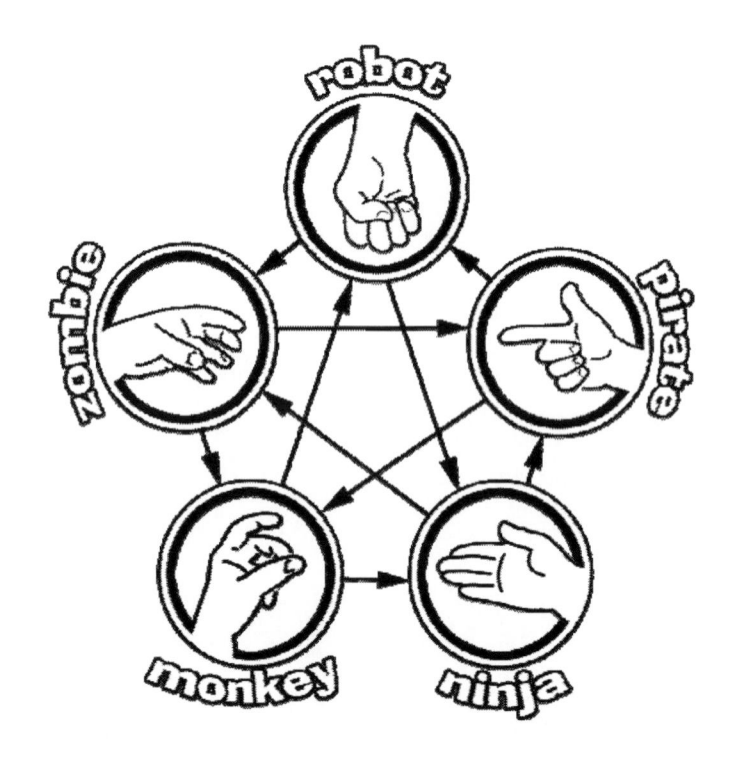

Fabulist Satire

It's worth noting this short story was written several years before the Thor movie was even in production.

Rebranding Thor

"We're thrilled to have your account, but I'm afraid your numbers are down since our initial chat."

"You're kiddin' me," Thor said.

"I'm afraid not, and I don't want to sugar-coat it," the lead consultant said. "We always get our best results when we start with an honest appraisal of the landscape." She switched the projector on, and started her presentation: "According to our research, belief in you is down to less than a fraction of one percent."

"What?"

Thunder shook the conference room, knocking over glasses and the pitcher of water. The other consultants looked down, and the intern, Tiffany, bolted. (Whether in terror or to get a towel to clean up, Tiffany didn't say.)

The lead consultant remained standing, and kept her cool. She'd had tougher clients—all those movie people, for example. After waiting for the rumbling to stop, she cleared her throat and said: "I have good news, too."

She clicked to the next slide, and said, "If you look at the segmented audiences, you are way up in the head-banging power metal market, though we suspect they are just worshipping you for the clothes."

"Wait, what? For the clothes?"

"Yes, you still have the whole heavy metal thing going for you. Punk too. But the fact is, the numbers are up. Six percent of them believe you exist."

"Only six percent?"

"People just aren't as keen on your bleak Nordic attitude as they used to be. But, Thor — may I call you Thor?"

"Thor is fine."

"Thor. Great. At least you're still here, and we think we can improve your fan base significantly."

"What do you mean, still here?"

"You didn't know? Some of the other Norse gods are disappearing. Bragi evaporated just last week."

"What do you mean evaporated? He's the God of Poetry, damn it!"

"*Poetry*? Do you have any idea how irrelevant poetry is— I mean demographically? He's lucky he only disappeared last week. Once you drop below a critical level of awareness…" The lead consultant blew on her fingers, and spread them apart. "Poof. I mean, nobody even knew about Bragi, except some scholars and Dungeons & Dragons freaks."

"How *am* I doing with the D&D crowd?" Thor asked.

"Yes, I'm glad you brought that up. That's on the next slide. Look! An increase of 15 percent in prayer—not fervent, and not authentic, of course, but at least it's *simulated* prayer."

"Still, what a bunch a poindexters."

"Sure, sure. However, let's be positive. Remember we're looking for a *platform* to build our branding efforts on." She brightened: "Julie from our entertainment division has some *great* news."

Julie took the remote from the lead consultant, and

opened the next deck of slides.

"What the hell is that?" Thor grunted.

"That is the cover of *The Mighty Thor #160*."

"A comic book? Is that supposed to be me? I never wore tights. By my hammer, why am I wearing a freakin' red cape?"

"It was the 60s."

"What does this have to do with me?"

"Because Marvel makes movies out of comics, and *Thor* is in production!" Julie said. She was enthusiastic, but nervous. (It was her first time pitching.)

"So?"

"Movies are *big*. Think of the *platform*. I hope they can get Matt Damon to play you."

"Will it make more people start worshipping me?"

Julie was as chirpy as they get, but that threw her. There was an awkward silence as she considered what kind of delusional freakazoid would start worshipping a character in a movie.

"Um, remember that what we're going for here is awareness," the lead consultant jumped in.

Julie rallied: "Like… you've got a day named after you!"

"Yeah, but nobody remembers that Thursday is named for me," Thor brooded. Thunder rumbled and some of the other consultants looked up, emboldened either by the passing storm of Thor's wrath, or perhaps Julie's inexorable perkiness.

Thor stood up, and lifted his hammer. "Look, isn't there *anything* I can do?" Thor asked. Even holding his mighty hammer, Mjolnir, he hated how whiny he sounded. If only he could just go back to Midgard and bust some heads!

"Of course there is! We love the hammer, by the way, and we're already in talks with Mike Holmes about getting you a guest spot on his renovation show."

"It's not that kind of hammer," Thor said. "It's for fighting giants and world-eating snakes. It throws freakin' lightning bolts!"

"Sure, sure, but what if we bring the inherent sexiness of fighting monsters to the home improvement industry?"

"Like, imagine you threw lightning bolts to demolish an old busted up home, and then you and Mike magically rebuilt a new house in the same day," Julie chirped.

"You want me to build houses?" Thunder shouted, and an ear-splitting clap of thunder shook the room. Several consultants bolted. The remaining PR people contemplated the table— even Julie.

"Okay, it doesn't have to be home renovation. Comic books, movies, TV shows, promoting Thursday as the go-to day of the week — these are just *ideas* at this point. The critical thing is that we have to get you out there. You need to get in the public's consciousness, especially since a certain deity has such a stranglehold on public awareness—"

"That shit Yahweh."

"Yep," the lead consultant confirmed.

"He's Allah too, remember. And just 'God' to the Christians. Our research shows even agnostics kind of dig him," Julie said.

"Yahweh has problems," the lead consultant said. "His numbers are down in Europe, and a significant percentage of his people are killing themselves in his name."

"Nice… wait, what's wrong with that?" Thor asked.

"He's just not happy about the optics of it; I mean, he's not really in favor of the sex thing, and these suicide bombers are mostly doing it for the virgins."

"Virgins?"

"Yeah, they've been promised virgins in the afterlife."

Thor was thoughtful. "That's a much better promise than the whole Ragnarök thing."

The lead consultant smiled. "Why don't we start with getting rid of Ragnarök, and promoting something just a little more positive.

"And our intern Tiffany has some fabulous ideas for your Facebook profile."

Proof of Kang's Corollary: Doug's Disaster

Doug was freaked out.

Global warming was going to melt his face (right after it killed all the polar bears and drowned the Maldives). It was a maxim that terrorists or free-roaming gun-nuts would board his bus and either blow it up, or shoot him with a semi-automatic. And if those disasters didn't strike, it was only a matter of time before he was felled by **BIRD FLU**!!

He could read it right there in the headlines. It was on the radio. The TV. It was inevitable. Doug was going to catch **BIRD FLU** and die. He wasn't on the priority list, and then it would be too late.

Then a happy thought struck him. None of that had happened. And wasn't there some kind of Swine Flu scare just a couple of years ago? He never caught that …

What if there was some sort of inverse relationship to disaster and the amount of fear churned up by the media: the more ink and airtime devoted, the less likely there would be a disaster?

It was a reassuring thought, and for the first time in many months, Doug didn't feel freaked out. He felt safe. That was probably why he didn't look before crossing the road to catch his transfer.

And that was when the bus struck him.

Pirate Therapy

Laurence arrived a few minutes late for his regular Thursday morning session.

From behind the door of his therapist's office, he heard a blood-curdling scream, and then a thump. A door opened somewhere, and Laurence heard a strange sound, almost as though something heavy was being dragged. He heard grunts, scraping, and the rhythmical percussion of something booming on the floor. Laurence looked around, and realized the secretary was not there. He also realized he was standing, tense.

The door to his therapist's office creaked opened, and he heard a rough voice shout: "Ahoy, Larry! Be ye out there laddie?"

"Uh. Yes."

"Come in, matey."

Laurence walked unsteadily to the door.

A pirate sat in his therapist's chair. He had wild, unkempt hair held in by a greasy red bandanna, and a full dreadlocked beard that looked like it was made out of black steel wool. He was wearing a stained white silk shirt, a sash of what was probably once a lovely dark green silk and pantaloons. He had one black boot, and he was missing a leg, which was replaced by a wooden peg that was carved into the shape of …

Laurence looked away.

"Arr matey, don't ye like me leg?"

"Uh, it's very creative," Laurence said. "Um. Um, where is Dr. Glick?"

"She's in-dee-sposed," the pirate said. "She's asked me to take care of her sessions today. Now, repeat after me: Arrrr!"

"Ar?"

"No, like ye mean it. Take a deep breath. No, don't sit down. Ye won't be sitting down this morning Larry, ye'll be workin'! Now, say it: Arrrr!!!"

"Arr."

"Avast!" the pirate stood, the obscenely rounded end of his peg leg booming on the floor. A cutlass lay on Dr. Glick's desk, and he picked it up. "I want to hear a real pirate yawlp before ye leave, ye bilge rat!"

Larry suddenly understood what that dragging sound had been. He looked around wildly for a weapon to defend himself; he picked up a pillow from the couch.

"Would ye like a blankie too, Larry? I won't be caring if ye need to carry around a stuffed bear, as long as I hear ye. Now take a deep breath, and say it: Arrrr!" The pirate's voice was incredibly loud. Laurence dropped the pillow and held his ears. He started shaking.

The pirate took a step closer and pointed the cutlass tip at Laurence's throat; he lowered his voice and said menacingly: "I've slit the throats of better men than ye, Larry me boyo. Now say it, smartly lad, smartly!"

"Arr!" Larry managed, terror driving his voice several octaves higher.

"Grand! Grand!" the pirate enthused. "Now, let's pretend ye got a pair, and say it again."

"Arrr!" Larry shouted.

"Again!"

"Arrr!"

"Again! Louder!"

"Arrr!" Larry screamed.

"Arrr!" the pirate joined in.

"Arrr! Arrr!"

"Arrrrr…….." Their joint shouting tailed off, and Laurence realized that the pirate was grinning at him.

"So how do ye feel, matey?"

Laurence wanted to say he felt good, but he know that wasn't the right answer, so he just muttered: "Arrrrr."

Restraint

You are walking down the street, minding your own business when a strange vehicle, driven by some kind of diminutive fish pulls up next to you. The vehicle is roughly half your size. You feel a pinprick of pain in your neck, and then, you black out.

You come to, briefly, to discover that you are immobilized, held in a net, and somehow, thousands of feet above your city. It is a disorienting, emotionally distressing moment and you pass out again.

When you awake, you find yourself in a small cell, roughly the size of a large handicapped washroom. There is enough room to take a couple of paces and turn around. You are not claustrophobic, but you now understand the phobia. All the sides of your new home are enclosed in glass, beyond which you can see little. The good news is the top of your cell is open to the sky. That is also bad news, because it is raining.

One of the tiny fish creatures is sitting on top of the cell, its mechanical legs dangling over the edge. It starts to make noises, which sound a little like crickets, or perhaps clicks. You realize the noise is coming from a miniature speaker, when you see its head is enclosed in some kind of diving helmet. It has strange prosthetic arms and legs, which you believe are called waldos. *What is this bizarre little cyborg-fish?* you think. It throws something at you. You almost missed it, it was so small, and then you realize it's part of a cheeseburger. Not even a bite. You let it sit on the ground.

It chatters some more at you through the speakers. You ignore it. It jumps on your shoulders, straddling your neck with its bizarre little waldo-legs. The chattering rises in intensity, and you try to ignore it. Several hours pass, and a half-dozen pieces of cheeseburger are lobbed at you. You ignore them all, and lift the creature off your back. You place it on the wall, where the chattering rises in intensity. Eventually, the sun sets, and the thing leaves.

You try to escape, but the cell is just high enough that you cannot pull yourself out. The glass is too thick to be kicked in, besides which, you think there might be nothing but water beyond the glass walls.

That night, you fall asleep curled in one corner of your new home, wondering what the hell is going on, and what this is all about. You awake the next morning, ravenous. You also need to relieve yourself, and you realize there is no facility for this in the tiny cell, even if it is the size of a public toilet. There is no choice, really.

The creature returns, and throws another piece of cheeseburger at you. This morsel you eat hungrily. As you gulp it down, you realize you've never felt so hungry, nor been so thirsty. It chatters some more, pointing to your left. Perhaps it wants you to move that way? *If I move that way, will it give me a drink of water? Or the whole cheeseburger?* You hope so, and so you move that way. Another morsel is thrown at you.

The morning passes in this productive manner, and just when you think you're going to die of thirst, another little fish-waldo creature — you've decided to call them Baldos, because of their hairless bodies — has some kind of argument with the first one. A hose appears at the top of the cell, and water trickles out. You drink from it. You had never felt so thirsty.

After this paltry drink, the chattering and cheeseburger bits return. You keep trying to comply, because let's face it, the only way you're going to keep up your energy enough to escape is to eat those little bits of cheeseburger.

You start to understand what hell is.

The day passes in a blur of bits of cheeseburger and chattering. The idiotic little thing jumps on your neck again, and you get that you're supposed to jump up and down while it's there, so you do. Another trickle of water and cheeseburger bits arrive. After the little creature and its companion leave (the Baldo with the water), you try pulling yourself up out of the cell again, but you realize it's just not going to happen. If anything, you're weaker than you were the day before.

That night you have trouble finding a place to lie down that isn't covered in your own bodily wastes, or bits of cheeseburger. Nothing is free of at least a skim of water. After a good cry, you fall asleep.

Several more days ensue, in a similar pattern, and after a week, you feel that tell-tale pinprick. This time, though, you realize you're merely tranquilized; you watch absently as a crew of the tiny creatures comes into your cell via a miniature door — a gush of water comes with it — and they clean the cell. Not really well, but they do clear out the worst of it. (You have designated one corner as "the latrine", and you're happy to see they concentrate their efforts there.)

The next day, you discover can see through the walls of the cell quite well. Beyond it are rows of the little dudes, except none of them are wearing the arm and leg waldos. Your buddy, the chattering asshole in the waldo, appears at the top of the cell and gets all the fish excited about something. It motions for you to come over, and you do, hoping to get a bit of cheeseburger. You're starving. And dying for salad. But never mind. If there's food on offer, you're game.

It jumps on your back and you jump up and down, and the tiny whales on the other side of the glass move their heads up and down. You wonder what that means, and think, *maybe it's applause*.

And then you realize you're on show. Some kind of terrestrial show for these marine motherfuckers. And that's when you grab the creature on your back, rip off its waldo arms and legs (you may have got a fin in there, though it wasn't really your intention) and its diving helmet, and drop it on the bottom of your cell. (Yes, in the "latrine".)

The head-bobbing on the other side of the glass stops, and it looks like you've caused quite the sensation. The crowd splits as fast as a crowd of fish can.

When the other Baldos appear on the top of cell, you

pirate therapy ∘ 75

reach up and crush them. More appear at the tiny door in your cell, water gushing in, and you step on them easily as they try to get to your trainer, who is suffocating in your shit.

Another group appears at the top of the cell, but before you can grab them, there is another pinprick of pain.

And then a kind of freedom.

Forgotten Bands of the Austrian Music Scene

Though they were best known for their aggressive neo-fascist jazz stylings of classic Tyrolian folk tunes, *The Pillage People* were equally popular with a certain sect of gigantic silly hat fetishists. (You know who you are.)

The members of the band: Amanda Uhgenkitz (flugelhorn and pistol), Bertrand "Stumpy" Russell (sousaphone, vocals and umbrella), Dennis "Don't Mind the Finger" Travesty (vocals and thermite grenade), Velaquez Eatme (guitar and pointed stick with razor attached to the end with duct tape), and Karl "The Beard" Marks (pocket xylophone, clarinet with flame attachment, and dictatorship of the proletariat).

Now, though they outsold the proto-fascist jazz stylings of *The Pillage People* four-to-one, the *Über-Musik Boys* never quite managed to make the big time.

This is unfair, particularly since they started the whole Lederhosen Thrash scene. Never able to break into the big time (Munich's beer halls), most of them had to take on menial jobs milking goats and persecuting small animals to make ends meet.

Young Adolf, in particular, was embittered.

Batman Lashes Out at the Other Members of the Justice League of America After Spending the Weekend at the Jack Nicholson Film Festival

You know, I'm getting a little tired of all the snide remarks about the way I fight crime.

We live in a world that has villains, and those villains have to be defeated by men with Batarangs. Or superpowers, if you've got them. (Yeah, and women too; don't get your star-spangled knickers in a knot, Wonder Woman.) I have a greater responsibility than you could possibly fathom. You weep for the psychotic killer that I sent to the hospital last night, and you curse my "methods". You have that luxury.

Green Lantern, you can always capture crooks with that weird radiation from your alien ring. And you, Wonder Woman, I wonder if that golden truth-telling lasso is as innocuous as it looks? You have easy options.

You know that when I beat that punk to within an inch of his life, while tragic for him, I saved lives. And my existence, while grotesque and incomprehensible to you, saves lives. I find it particularly ironic that you, Martian Manhunter, find me grotesque, but you do, don't you, you green uni-browed freak!

I'll grant my methods are extreme, but they work. You people with your superpowers don't dare admit it. You don't want the truth because deep down in places you don't talk about at parties, you want me cruising the streets of Gotham in my Batmobile, you need me in my Batmobile! Who *else* is going to clean up that hellhole?

I use words like discipline and detective work and a lot

of made-up words starting with "Bat". I use these words as the backbone of a life spent intimidating the criminal classes. You use them as a punchline. I have neither the time nor the inclination to explain myself to you, who succeed because of the detective work that I provide, and then question the manner in which I provide it. I would rather you just said thank you, and went on your way. Otherwise, I suggest you pick up a Batarang and solve a few crimes without your superpowers.

Either way, I don't give a damn what you think is "excessive" or "brutal" or "verging on insane".

And you Superman — you are such a polished ass kisser that it takes my breath away. How dare you let Hal raise this issue, when you are just as tough on the thugs we fight as me! You break more bones with your love taps than I do with my Bat-ido.

Do you have any idea how hard I have to work just to be *considered* a superhero? All you do is fly around in the freaking pajamas your mommy sent you to Earth in and you're the darling of the media. You're only special because of our sun — you're just the product of our environment.

I don't want to be a product of our environment. I want our environment to be a product of *me*. Years ago there were no superheroes. That was only you and me, Clark — we had each other. We were real head-breakers, true vigilantes. We took over our cities! And twenty years after the time when a superhero couldn't be taken seriously, we have the JLA, and we rule this planet! And that's what the "normies" don't realize. If I've got one thing against the "normies", it's this — no one gives it to you. You have to take it.

And you, Wonder Woman. I know you think I'm a "normie". I don't have any god-given super-human powers. All I have is my intellect, my inventions, and my iron will. I'm a goddamn marvel of modern science. If Barry was here, he would tell you. He used to be a "normie" before he vibrated himself to death! Stop smirking, Wonder Woman!

Now, I'm going to back to Gotham City. Always brings a smile to my face . . .

And Aquaman, I haven't forgotten you. There are two kinds of angry people — explosive and implosive. Explosive is the type of individual you see screaming at the cashier for not taking his coupon. Implosive is the cashier who remains quiet day after day and then finally shoots everyone in the store.

You're the cashier, Aquaman. Probably at a fish market. And instead of shooting them, you'd get the lobsters to pinch their asses.

If this story seems familiar, it's because this is a retelling of the Bros. Grimm classic.

The Blue Light, 2011

After his injury in the war, his leaders told the soldier, "thanks for your service, but we don't need you anymore." The soldier was sent home, without much help, or rehab, and no occupation, that was for sure. So he got work doing odd jobs for an economist; some days he'd dig holes, other days he'd pick up garbage at the side of the road and sell it to the economist. It was just enough to live on, but not enough to improve his situation.

Then one day the economist said, "I have this blue light I need you to bring me, and if you do that, I'll make sure you're set up comfortably for life. The only thing is it's kind of hard to get at — you'll have to crawl through a tunnel to an underground cave to find it."

The financial wizard didn't mention the underground dwellers who lived off rats, and fungus, and the occasional servant that he had sent down in his previous attempts to recover the light. But the soldier had been trained in battle, and he brought his shovel with him, so he was able to defend himself, and find the blue light.

It was easy to see in the darkness of the cave; its ethereal glow could be seen from the far end, like a dawn. And when he got there, he was delighted to discover that it held the secrets of the economist, and his leaders, and what's more, all the people who had any kind of wealth or power. It was a treasure trove of information.

When he got to the surface, the economist asked him if he found the blue light, and the soldier said, "No, sorry, it wasn't down there."

So the economist fired him, but the soldier didn't care, because now he knew where the economist kept his hoard of gold. Which he took.

The soldier could have retired comfortably on that, but he was just getting started.

Pastafarianism, or the Church of the Flying Spaghetti Monster, is a satirical religion begun to protest the decision by a school board in Kansas to teach intelligent design as an alternative to evolution. It purports that god is an invisible flying spaghetti monster that created the universe. It also suggests that global warming is caused by the dearth of pirates. Ridiculous.

The Norse Pastafarian Saga

New Sect Believes It Is Vikings, not Pirates, That Cause Global Warming

LONDON, ONTARIO (The Skwib) — The first schism within the Pastafarian religion has appeared in the sleepy Canadian city of London, Ontario, and it is led by the charismatic preacher Dr. Maximilian Tundra.

"Other worshippers of the Flying Spaghetti Monster have claimed that it is the declining number of pirates that have caused the increase in global warming, hurricanes and earthquakes. In truth it is the shortage of Vikings that has caused these ills, indeed, most of our problems are because we lack Vikings," Dr. Tundra, the self-proclaimed Prophet of the Pasta, told The Skwib.

Tundra is an unlicensed physician, best known for his avant-garde work in the pharmaceutical and plastic surgery industries. Though he does not come from an evangelical background, Tundra has gathered an impressive number of worshippers of the Great Pasta.

"I have communed with the Great Pasta at length," Tundra said, "and it has told me that we must produce more Vikings or the Earth is doomed. It also said that I should really reduce my peyote button intake."

The breakaway sect, called the Norse Pastafarians, have suggested that the false religion fell into the trap of thinking it was pirates that have caused so many disasters because they do not take a "long, historical view" of human history. They also do not believe in redundancy.

When asked if there would soon be a "mongol horde" version of Pastafarianism, Tundra ran away, shouting: "I cannot say more — the Lord has told me you are on the South Beach Diet!"

An Interview With Religious Leader, Dr. Maximilian Tundra

The Skwib: Thank you, Dr. Tundra, for finally agreeing to chat with us about your controversial new sect of Pastafarianism. Could you explain to our readers, in case they don't already know, what are the differences between your group and other Pastafarians?

Dr. Tundra: You're welcome. Well, as you know, Pastafarianism is about worshiping the great Flying Spaghetti Monster (FSM), in all its noodley goodness. In most respects we follow the teachings of its Prophet, Bobby Henderson, but in one important aspect, we differ. We believe it is Vikings, not pirates that cause the multitude of ills that affect us: global warming, earthquakes, hurricanes, and other natural disasters.

So, naturally, instead of wearing full pirate regalia, we like to trick ourselves out in Viking gear.

The Skwib: Yes, I was going to say that is a very impressive horned helmet you are wearing. My understanding is that it's a myth that Vikings wore them, though.

Dr. Tundra: It's true — the historical Vikings rarely wore them, and we would never wear them if we were going into battle. But the FSM said we should make it easy to see we were the true religion.

The Skwib: Are there any other differences between you and the pirate-loving Pastafarians?

Dr. Tundra: Oh, we love pirates too, but they obviously are not the cause of global warming. Much of our new creed is still being revealed to me by the Great Pasta. But we believe other modern mysteries are caused by the lack of Vikings too. The increased number of orphaned socks, for example.

Now, one of the first missions of the First Church of the Noodley Norsemen is to increase our numbers.

The Skwib: Really, the Noodley Norsemen?

Dr. Tundra: We're still working on the name for our Church. What matters is that we follow the Prophet's teachings.

The Skwib: So what drew you to Pastafarianism in the first place?

Dr. Tundra: Initially, I was drawn to the flimsy moral standards, but I also like the Friday religious holiday.

The Skwib: So you got into it for crass personal reasons? We note that you have had a rather suspect career. Is it true that you have lost your licence to practise medicine?

Dr. Tundra: Ah, ah, I'm having a vision ...

The Skwib: And is it also true that you have a, shall we say, somewhat *avant garde* approach to the use of pharmaceuticals?

Dr. Tundra: The Great Pasta is speaking to me ... O' ramen pasta yum! O' ramen pasta yum!

Ex-media: Dr. Tundra Hits His Peak

He had been lost for many days — perhaps as many as forty, he wasn't sure — but one thing was certain, he had reached the highest point that he could climb without proper equipment. Dr. Maximilian Tundra was uncertain why he had decided to climb up, instead of down, when he got separated from his trekking group in the Annapurna Himalayas. But he was glad that he had, because he wasn't alone anymore.

He sensed a presence, no, capital P — Presence — with him as he sat on a house-sized boulder about 3,000 feet above the base camp of Annapurna I.

While he watched the avalanches rumble nearly a mile

above him on the mountain, he saw a light, which grew in intensity as it seemed to come towards him. As the light got brighter, Dr. Tundra thought that he could see a figure within it, and he felt a sudden stab of fear.

"Max?" a voice asked him.

"Yes? Who is this?"

"Who do you think it is, Max?"

"Well, either chronic hypoxia has messed up my temporo-parietal junction and the prefrontal cortex of my brain, or you're God."

"Can't it be both, Max?"

"Sure, why not? Of course, social deprivation may be causing prefrontal lobe dysfunction, and lowering my inhibitions. And let's be honest, God. They weren't that high to begin with."

"You're speaking of your peyote addiction."

"Yes."

"And your dalliance with that made-up religion, Norse Pastafarianism."

"I still like the idea that Vikings are the cause of all our problems," Dr. Tundra admitted.

"Perhaps they are," the voice suggested.

"Really?"

"Yes, and perhaps you should get serious about letting everyone know."

"Cool. And God? Why don't you look like spaghetti?"

Suddenly, the figure turned into a large bowl, filled with pasta in long slender strips and an aromatic Bolognese sauce; it was wearing a horned Viking helmet. From within the noodles, the voice said, "Because I am linguini. Now spread the word."

Interlude

Lucidiva™ — Side effects

Common side effects include heavy breathing, panting, hyperventilation, lack of peripheral vision, excessive screaming, painful hearing and nasal discharge that may look like rice pudding. Sorry, but it happens.

You should probably enjoy flatulence if you want to take this drug, unless you live at an even-numbered address, in which case, expect projectile vomiting on an hourly basis. Married men can expect long periods of impotence, though we have not conclusively proved this is because of the drug.

Single men in the company of nuns should be ready for painful, humiliating bouts of extreme priapism. Women will want to have a razor handy. (For the excessive hair growth, not for dealing with priapism.)

If you're thinking about taking this drug while driving, just stop right there. Also, most people taking this drug find themselves incapable of walking, crawling or singing the works of Cole Porter. Gershwin is okay.

Rare side effects include basket weaving, frequent urination, syncopated urination, explosive urination and occasionally, uncontrolled urination. We recommend you set up an IV to replace your bodily fluids BEFORE you take your first dose. You may also want to begin your Lucidiva™ in the bathtub, or public pool.

Speaking of your first dose, when you begin taking Lucidiva™, you will experience clarity of thought and eloquence of speech that makes President Obama look like his predecessor. We apologize to everyone studying for an MBA, but clearly Lucidiva™ is not for you.

If your skin begins to strobe, consult your physician. If you fingernails burst into flame, put them out, but not with water. That will not work. Trust us on this. We've tested this extensively. Use baking powder, or some kind of halon system. Just hold your breath if using the latter. If you happen to inhale halon while taking Lucidiva™ we cannot be held responsible. Just make sure your will is up to date and your house is fully insured.

Very rarely, patients experience visions of aliens, talking monkeys and sometimes, angels. If the latter, it is acceptable to consult a priest.

Finally, if you see the six-foot bird, don't try to talk to it. Don't even —

Ask General Kang: Grooming, Fashion & Personal Advice

I have a hot date tonight — should I wear boxers or briefs?

The General can tell you're a guy. Only a human male would frame the question in such a crass way. What you're asking, essentially, is how you should prepare yourself for having sexual congress with this hypothetical human female. In The General's opinion, this event seems to have a high degree of improbability.

The very fact that you're asking an interstellar overlord who is, without stretching the facts, a superior being but nevertheless of a different species entirely tells The General something.

Sorry to interrupt, but are you speaking about yourself in the third person?

Yes, it makes The General sound more distant and authoritative. However, when it comes to human females, The General is not an authority. What The General does know is that human females value power and wealth. And if you live in North America, then they also like their men to have a sense of humor.

Therefore, I suggest gold-plated, kevlar briefs, with some kind of laser defence array — this will demonstrate both your power and financial wherewithal — and perhaps you could get the goldsmith to engrave some kind of happy face or something comical on the exterior, thus showing your lighter, humorous side.

Even better — in the seat have your engineers build-in a whoopee cushion. That's always a hit with the ladies.

How Do I Keep My New Year's Resolutions?

We had a similar custom on my homeworld, Neecknaw, but there we called them Slorg Wishes.

Slorg was once the Overlord of our planet, back in the Taupe Ages — he was known colloquially as the Beige Lord, but he was actually quite a colorful character.

Every year, he would wish that he could make something better about the people who worked for him. For Bluknark the Compulsive Eater (Minister of Celebrations and Public Executions), Slorg required that he lose some of his massive monkey gut. For the Minister of War and Love, Lord Prangdong, Slorg required fewer paternity suits. And so on.

And then the next year, Slorg would review their progress during his Annual Performance Evaluation Festival. (Known amongst the commoners as the APE-fest.) If you did not achieve your goals, then Slorg exacted some kind of punishment, depending on how badly you missed the mark. The aforementioned Bluknark actually gained weight one year, and he was fed to the Almighty Cram-Beast, and is presumably still being digested. Though Ministers were held to a higher standard, everyone was terrified of not meetings Slorg's Wishes.

If you succeeded, that was called "Meeting Expectations" and you were only lightly tasered, right before the Breakfast after APE-fest. (This kept costs down because people were usually not too hungry then.) Naturally, the following year's Slorg Wishes were quite a bit more onerous, because if a tool like you could meet your goals, then clearly, they weren't challenging enough.

My suggestion is that you engage me as your Slorg. I have my own taser and everything.

I'm in high school. How I can improve my self-esteem?

Some researchers will tell you that self-esteem is heavily influenced by things you will have no control over, such as your looks, and how "cool" you are seen to be by your peers. And popularity too.

Now, if I'd let such trifles get in my way, I never would have conquered most of the known galaxy. You may not know it to look at me, particularly you hairless humans, but for an über-chimp, I'm somewhat less hirsute than the Neecknabian ideal.

And in high school, I looked positively glabrous. That might be a good thing in Hollywood gay bars, but at Commander Chee-bee High, not good. (Commander Chee-bee was the Hero of the Spider Wars, inventor of the "brush and flush" battle maneuver, for those of you not up on the glorious history of Planet Neecknaw.) But did I obsess over the patches of skin you could see through my thin layer of hair?

Of course I did! It was high school.

But I used it. I drove the rage deep inside and it helped me overcome the Neecknabian Senate, using nothing but guile, a bathtub filled with depilatory, and several squads of insanely loyal, bald gorilloids with halitosis and broadswords. (Later these stalwarts became the Gorilloids-with-Fezzes Brigade.)

When I was undisputed master of all of Planet Neecknaw, my old high school chums understood who was popular, and who wasn't.

Then the forced shavings began.

What is your policy re: instant gratification?

I'm totally against it.

From what I can see there is too much instant gratification happening here on Terra, and this is at least some part of the reason why I'll conquer this world soon.

I'm a fan of a system of gratification we call *The Rectitude* on my home world.

The Rectitude started out as a philosophical movement of neo-utopian bonobos, but it eventually caught on within the simian population at large, and I hope that someday it will catch on amongst the primates of this world too.

What is The Rectitude?

It sounds kind of proctologist-y, but essentially, to have some kind of physical gratification, the idea is that first you have to earn it. (Yes, just go ahead, say it just like John Houseman.)

The best kind of *Rectitude* to earn is through intense physical effort. For example, if you climb a mountain, that earns you lots of *Rectitude* — at least a week of all kinds of debauchery. Walk to the store instead of driving, and that probably earns you enough *Rectitude* to eat the Cheese Doodles you were going to inhale in the first place.

Once Earth is fully under my control, every sentient being on the planet can look forward to a lifetime of earning and expending *Rectitude*.

Stop groaning! It will be good for you humans to learn a little self-discipline!

Science Fictional Meanderings

How Anne of Green Gables Destroyed the World

"Like most of you I was inclined to say the war was caused by fish, but ultimately, I blame Anne of Green Gables," Cadman Michaels, alternate historian, told the learned audience at the annual History of World War Three Conference.

"After a close examination of the evidence, I can say now with some confidence that the roots of World War III could be found in a red-haired fictional character, and three quintessentially Canadian things: beer, ice hockey, and something called Tim Hortons' coffee," said Michaels, who held doctorates in theoretical physics and history.

"My extensive work in multi-universal alternative histories, made possible by my invention, the Moorcock Inter-Dimensional Time Inversion Tunneller (MIDTIT), shows the cause of the war was actually much earlier in history, well before the breakup of Canada. I intend to outline this series of events in this presentation."

There were grumbles from the learned audience at the annual conference, held in sunny and (relatively) radiation-free Blenheim, NZ. The MIDTIT was controversial technology, but several papers had proved its efficacy at determining historical turning points.

"I'd have to say the turning point was an incident in 1972, during the so-called Summit Series, an ice hockey match played between Canadian NHL players and the Russian Red Army team. Prior to the sixth game, played at the Luzhniki Palace of Sports in Moscow, Russian officials "lost" a shipment of beer the Canadian team had been expecting. Few other historians have noted how grumpy this made the Canadian players, and in particular, Bobby Clarke. "

The audience stared at Michaels blankly.

"Clarke was the player who slashed Valeri Kharlamov's ankle, fracturing it; this took him out of the next game, and made him ineffective for the final game."

"Wait, that's not true!" someone from the audience shouted.

"Exactly," someone else said, Michaels thought it was Hans Gruber, Professor of Pre-Radiation Sports at the University of New Heidelberg, in Perth Australia. "Kharmalov played brilliantly in the remaining games, which is how the Russian team took the series four games to three, with one tie."

"Ah," Michaels smiled. "You are right of course. I've been telling you about the alternative history. Now, the other surprise I have for you is actual images of this alternative history, taken by a recording device that can utilize the inter-dimensional tunnel created by the MIDTIT."

He played several minutes of grainy, black and white video, showing the events he described, including the Canadian victory in game eight.

"My apologies for the quality of the video, but for some reason, I can only capture video and stills from sources broadcast during the time period the MIDTIT is examining."

This produced fewer grumbles, but a higher level of chatter in the room.

"I agree. It is fascinating, yes? In this alternative history, the Canadians win the Summit Series, and unlike our own timeline, this prevents the country from falling apart. We have always thought the Canadian experiment failed because it was a historical necessity. When you look at the absurd country, there was very little to hold it together, given the regional differences, an active separatist movement in Quebec, Western alienation, and the pressure from the United States. But imagine if Canada wins the Summit Series …"

Terry McDonaldson, who was born in Winnipeg, Manitoba, when it was part of the defunct country called Canada, and who actually played "ice hockey" as it was called in New Auszealand, could be heard whispering, "Beauty, eh?"

"But my examination of this timeline has shown that it would take more than Canadian ascendency in ice hockey to keep the country together. It required coffee. In particular, a brand of coffee called Tim Horton's coffee."

"That's absurd," Gruber said.

"No, it's true. I can show you the figures, but first, let me show you a series of current day advertisements in this timeline. I recorded this yesterday."

Michaels played beautifully crisp video showing a father taking his son to an early morning hockey game, and stopping — before and after the game — at a Tim Horton's to buy coffee and donuts.

"What are those things?" someone asked.

"They are called donuts. They're made, essentially, out of fried dough — which is made from wheat."

"I remember wheat," someone else said. The few Soviet historians who had survived the war shifted uncomfortably in their seats. It had been their government that destroyed all wheat with a biological weapon.

"They look good," Hans Gruber said.

"Yes, I'm sure they were and are delicious, in that universe," Michaels agreed. "The point is, the Canadian people had this institution to help keep them together. Fueled by Tim Horton's coffee and their delectable fried dough, Canadians had the energy and élan to keep their country together, unlike in our own sad timeline. But without the popularity of hockey, Tim Horton's (founded by a famed hockey player) would never have achieved such success as a franchise."

"But you said you would show how the war was caused by Anne of Green Gables," the Winnipegger, Tory McDonaldson said.

"Right. I did. So, now I have established that without two of Canada's greatest institutions — hockey (or ice hockey as we know it) and Tim Horton's — an offshoot of their hockey culture that bound them together — Canada could not stay together. Now, I ask you to remember your pre-war history. What happened in our timeline?" It was clearly a rhetorical question, so Michaels continued: "The country started to break up. First Quebec separated, and then Alberta. The first became independent and the second joined the US. Other provinces began to follow, as the US invited Ontario, BC, Saskatchewan, and Manitoba to join. They even asked New Brunswick, Newfoundland and Nova Scotia. They all were absorbed by the US.

"All except little Prince Edward Island; we now know that it was just an oversight by the State Department. Nobody noticed the tiny province on the map. But this lack of geographic acumen would lead inevitably to the destruction of a global civilization."

People were nodding their heads. He had them now with this familiar material.

"PEI, justifiably outraged and upset that they had been ignored by the United States, declared that they were de facto, now Canada, and moved the federal capital to Charlottetown. (As an interesting footnote, this is where the country had its beginnings too.) They also declared that as the government of Canada, they retained the vastness of the Yukon and the Northwest Territories. There were ominous complaints from both the US government and the new Quebec government, though really, most of the Quebec troops were engaged in a civil war with the aboriginal peoples of Quebec, so they were not a threat. The US most definitely was, so PEI — sorry, Canada –"

There were chuckles throughout the room.

"– looked for allies. And as we all know, they found Japan. All the textbooks say the Japanese recognized that if PEI — sorry, Canada — became a protectorate of Japan so it would have access to the rich fishing waters of not only the Gulf of St. Lawrence, but also all the Arctic waters surrounding the territories. The so-called Sushi Factor.

"And of course, there were other elements that led to war: seeing how happy it made everyone in the Canadian states, President Carter was forced to institute universal health care throughout all the United States during his second term; this, in turn, weakened the federal coffers so that when Ronald Reagan became president, he did not have the resources he needed to start a new arms race and bankrupt the Soviets, as he planned. (Incidentally, I'm working on a video that will show how this played out in the other timeline I'm discussing.) Plus, Reagan had a whole new Cold War on his hands with the Japanese. Granted, the Japanese were a non-nuclear nation, but with the resources they were able to pull out of the oceans and the territories, it gave their economy the power to rival that of the US."

Most of these arguments were familiar to the audience, and he was starting to lose them again. "But I have evidence that shows the Japanese would not have taken over Canada — not even with the fish factor. I will play more video now, this from our own timeline. I'd also like to take this opportunity to introduce Dr. Akido Suzuki, who is one of the few surviving Japanese, to translate for me."

The video showed happy Japanese people, holding up placards. Suzuki translated: "The signs say, 'We love Anne', and 'Save Green Gables'." Then the video changed to the audience room in the palace of the Japanese emperor. He was speaking with his senior ministers. "The revered Emperor say his people love Anne of Green Gables. He say he understands the geopolitical danger this protectorate would put Japan in, but for the sake of his people, he asks his government to do it. He says that he would like to visit Green Gables too, but only if it is on Japanese soil."

The video ends.

"Say, where did you find that video?" Gruber asked. "No one has been able to get to Japan since the war. And as far as I know, any records that may have survived would be too radioactive to examine."

"Oh, I used the MIDTIT to record that conversation."

"Didn't you say you could only record transmissions from the period? Surely that wasn't ever telecast."

"The Emperor with his ministers?" Michaels said. "Of course not. No. I can only record broadcast signals from other timelines, inter-dimensionally. Our own universe I can record anything, anywhere."

"Even now?"

"No, I can't record something that is happening in the present moment. But I can record something that happened just a second ago," Michaels said.

There was a brief silence as the assembled historians absorbed the significance of this, including Michaels.

The room erupted in conversation, and Michaels realized that if there was going to be another war, he already had a good idea what — and who — would have caused it.

Pages I Have Dog-Eared in the Fall 2037 Hammacher Schlemmer Glaven Catalog

The Best Levitation Belt

This levitation belt earned The Best rating from the Hammacher Schlemmer Glaven Institute because it was the easiest to put on and operate while falling from a building. 48 out of 49 of our tests were successful. A levitation belt industry expert described The Best model's inertial dampening as "great and most dampening by far" because it was able to dampen terminal velocity to gravely injuring velocity with enough alacrity to save 48 Testing Drones from "street pizzafication". The Best Levitation Belt is also capable of *actual* levitation, if the inertial dampening dial is turned to "full" and the wearer jumps up in the air. The Best model allows wearers to levitate for several minutes, and prevents certain death from a single fall from up to a 20-storey building. It is highly recommended that the batteries be recharged after such use. Sizes: XS-XL. (Not recommended for larger sizes.)

The Thomas Kincaid Pop-Up Christmas Tree and Santa Virus Dispenser

This is a six-foot Christmas tree that pops up instantly and is pre-decorated with original artwork by renowned holiday artist Thomas Kincaid, all of which can dispense Viritron's patented Santa Virus™. The tree rises from a flat position in concentric circles to its full 30 inch width and 76 inch height, and simply hangs on the included stand, in which is embedded a Viritron Aerosol Dispensing Unit, capable of infecting anyone within a 200 foot radius of the tree with a virus that will guarantee you have good sales during the important holiday shopping season. Three hundred glistening clear lights are nestled among the branches and cast a warm glow on the 70 richly-painted globe ornaments, which will be sure to distract your customers from the brief intense psychic pain they will feel upon contact with the Santa Virus™, as it coerces them to buy more gifts than they can afford. The tree has two additional gold and burgundy ribbons, 15 velvet-like poinsettias, and a golden bow, which has a rebreather and a two-minute oxygen supply embedded in it, if you are inadvertently caught in your store while the tree is circulating the Santa Virus™. The tree collapses for easy storage during the off-season. (15lbs. Santa Virus sold separately.)

The Laser Equipped Autonomous Robotic Vacuum

This is the robotic vacuum that navigates autonomously through your home up to seven times per week, where it can either clean your floors or patrol for intruders. The unit's specially designed dual, counter-rotating agitator brushes spread carpet fibers and enable the vacuum to remove hair and other detritus from low- and high-pile carpets, while its dual Class VII lasers are capable of vaporizing any intruders (or more likely, unwanted refuse left on the floor). Sensors redirect the unit when it encounters furniture, walls, or stairs, and its anti-tangle technology reverses the rotation of the brushes when it encounters rug fringe. Sensors will also allow your pets to survive The Laser Equipped Autonomous Robotic Vacuum. It cleans up to four rooms, and incinerates up to three large intruders per charge, and automatically returns to its drive-on charger when its battery runs low. (2' 1/2" H x 13" Diam. 11 3/4 lbs.)

The Frozen Soylent Green Soft Serve Processor

This is the device that instantly turns Soylent Green and other flavorings into a soft-serve treat. The unit combines frozen Soylent Green and any additional Soylent products you can scavenge and instantly churns the ingredients to produce a treat with the texture of frozen yogurt or soft-serve ice cream, but without the crushing existential angst of eating people. The chute easily accepts Soylent Green, Soylent Red, Soylent Orange, and a wide variety of decomposing garbage; the integrated conical, spinning blade mashes and incorporates the nutrients into a silky-smooth confection. The chute, plunger, and blade are dishwasher safe. Includes a dessert storage container, four popsicle moulds, recipe booklet, and the number to the Soylent Suicide Promotion hotline. Plugs into AC. (14" H x 7 1/2" W x 6" D.)

The Cybernetic Thought Projection Hat

This hat recalls the iconic headgear worn by the Cognition Brigade during the Second Robotic War. First developed for long distance thought projection, hats of this design were worn by countless Thought Soldiers during the war; "Think Grunts" preferred the helmet for its ability to combat the medulla-inhibiting freeze rays of the Robotic Army of Dread. True to the originals, its buttery-soft, plasskin dendrite injectors are durable yet supple, and its genuine high-impact titanium exterior and classic sound-sealing ear covers provide comfort and the ability to mute the screams of the Thought Soldiers dying around you, or more likely, inane chatter in the office. This hat will allow you to send your thoughts up to one parsec away, assuming the person you're sending your thoughts to is also wearing a similar hat. The hat automatically shuts off when removed from the head, or when the head is removed from the neck. Sizes S, M, L and XL.

Memo to Hollywood: 9 time travel/pop culture mashups for derivative, yet original, TV-to-movie projects

1. Gilligan is marooned on "Más a Tierra", later renamed to Robinson Crusoe Island, with Alexander Selkirk, a Scottish castaway who has a low tolerance for bullshit.

2. Joey (from *Friends*) is sent back in time to live with the Fourth Earl of Sandwich, while the Earl is still working on his eponymous invention. (I recommend sending Joey back to the time when Sandwich is experimenting with cedar boards instead of bread.)

3. Don't remake *MASH*. Instead, transport all the characters of TV-series of *MASH* (season 7 or after) back to the *actual* Korean War. This is the first offering in a series of pop culture/war mashups, which could include:

    4. *McHale's Navy* at the Battle of Trafalgar

    5. *China Beach* at the Crimea

    6. *Hogan's Hero's* at the Battle of Gaugamela (put them on the Persian side for maximum laughs).

7. Jerry Seinfeld is sent to work at a medieval tannery in Sweinslop, Germany, without any sneaker polish.

8. Cliff Claven and Norm Peterson join the Donner Party.

9. The main cast of *Sex in the City* visits Krakatoa, in 1883, moments before it explodes with 13,000 times the force of the Hiroshima bomb.

The Sarcastic Cyborg Debriefs

[RECORDING STARTS]

Is this thing on?

Seriously. Is it on? I'm not getting any neural feedback.

You humans are so odd. You are human aren't you? Why don't you just implant a microphone in your skull — there's lots of room. That way the rest of the world could hear the same voice you do.

Oh yeah, **you** don't sound like that. Right. Everybody says that when they hear their recorded voice the first time. It's so predictable.

But just imagine what it was like for us before we improved the speaker systems in our bonded polycarbide armor — our voices always came out so screechy and monotone. Here, let me play you an old recording:

"EX-TER-MIN-ATE!"

Oh *that's* terrifying, isn't it?

I mean, if we had deep booming voices like that Darth Vader dude, it would be frightening. But as it was, we sounded like the Chipmunks after a crack cocaine and peyote button binge. Gonzo alien invasion.

Don't worry, I'd never probe *you*.

Of course I'm being sarcastic. That's what we do. We probe you bastards every chance we get. Not only is it fun, we know you hate it. (Well, *most* of you do.)

Frankly, we just can't trust a species that can survive without mechanical and electronic augmentation.

Well naturally, that's why we introduced the Internet to your planet. You don't think you apes came up with it do you? The iPod too.

What is wrong with you? Don't you understand sarcasm? Are you brain-damaged or something?

I'm sorry. You do work for the government, don't you?

I see you've discovered how to open my armor. Well, let me tell you, you're in for a surprise. Yes, I'm one of the most attractive women you've ever met Jimbo. I only use Sean Connery's voice pattern because it sounds cool whenever I use the letter 's'.

[MECHANICAL SIGH]

Yes, sarcasm again. I'm actually a little green blob, and the armor just makes me feel big. And shiny. Just like a forty-year-old account exec in his Hummer.

I see you've got the outer carapace open. Well, don't say I didn't warn you.

[RECORDING ENDS]

Why Dr. McCoy Was Not A Whiny Bitch

Everyone in the original Star Trek was quite condescending to Bones whenever he got fretful about using the transporter.

Yet Dr. McCoy had solid, philosophical reasons for being freaked out by the device. Basically, the transporter disassembles all your molecules, and then reassembles them somewhere else. (Assuming something doesn't go horribly wrong in the process, as it did in pretty much every other episode.)

It's an existentialist nightmare.

So that means when you voluntarily use the transporter, you're opting for death via de-atomization over a period of several agonizing seconds. Sure, a copy of you will go on, but who knows, maybe it will be the evil copy of you, or perhaps the machine will screw up, and you'll end up with Mr. Spock's wang protruding from your forehead. In either case, it doesn't really matter, because the you that *you are at this moment* (which granted, is also an illusion of sorts, but that's a subject for another time) is going to die. And presumably it hurts a bit to be de-atomized. Did anyone else ever think it took quite a long time for them to stop "sparkling"? It's seconds at least. Now imagine what that feels like, having your atoms ripped apart over a period of several seconds. Having trouble? Pluck out a few nose hairs. Now imagine that in every molecule of your body for several seconds.

His crewmates should have cut Bones a little slack; let him take the shuttlecraft if he wanted. Besides, when you're fighting Tiranglian Lizard people, or reprogramming a rogue computer, the doctor's only going to be helpful in stitching you up afterwards. (Or whatever "non-barbaric" technology" Dr. McCoy used.)

If anything, McCoy was pretty stoic about the whole

thing. If it had been me, there's no way you're getting me onto the transporter pad:

> "Mr. Rayner, put on your red shirt and step onto the transporter pad, we're going down to the surface," Kirk ordered the pudgy and pale-looking ensign.
>
> "Nuh-uh!"
>
> "Mr. Rayner, you're going down to the surface with the rest of the landing party, where we're all going to die. Well, you're going to die. Bones and Spock and I will be fine."
>
> "We all die every time we use the transporter!" Ensign Rayner cries.
>
> "Don't make me beat you."
>
> "Frankly ..." Mr. Rayner lifts shoulders. "I'd prefer that..." Mr. Rayner raises hands. "Jim." Mr. Rayner thrusts hands forward.
>
> Then Kirk decks him (ripping his shirt in the process).
>
> *Green-skinned dancing girls appear on the transporter pad and begin doing the Hippy Shake, while Spock raises an eyebrow.*

Interlude

The Rush of Heaven Downward

He was falling.

Once he'd stopped screaming like a fool, he'd spent at least a few seconds trying to figure out how much time he had. He couldn't really breathe. And it was cold. Without a computer it was hard to calculate, but he had at least a few minutes 'til the end. None of that was too awful.

He was never going to be near her again. Hear her laugh. Feel her hand caress his cheek. This was his pain. The image of her was in his mind as he fell.

The other end of the wormhole had appeared somewhere in the lower stratosphere. Not high enough that the low pressure killed him instantly, but high enough that it was lethally cold. When he had appeared, the earth looked distant below. Colors instead of shapes. He had no sensation of his increasing speed. It took some time falling before he started to hear the wind whistle around his outspread limbs; he was in the classic skydiver's pose, even though he'd never participated in the sport. The more surface area he could flatten against the air, the lower his terminal velocity. It could buy him seconds. Precious seconds to remember.

Thoughts of her warmed him, though the air was so bitter. His fingers felt like they might be frozen solid – he couldn't move them without terrible stabs of pain shooting up his arms. He let them be, and tried to keep his body level. It was hard to tell how fast he was going, but the clouds below rushed up so chillingly he had to remind himself they were made of water vapor, not solid earth.

That would come later.

The sound of the wind, louder now. He could breathe again. His mind filled with images, memories, a rapid-fire flickering that would shame even the most crazed music video director. She was there in many of them. There were so many days that were warm, and honest, and tinged with joy. It was beautiful.

He blasted through the top layer of cloud, thin cirrus that would look like mare's tails from the ground. Then he was through, and he could see the ground, still far below. At least a minute. He felt it now, the rush of heaven downward.

He supposed that he should feel foolish. After all the tests, there was really no guarantee that the wormhole would continue to open to safety. A least he hadn't appeared somewhere that ended it instantly. He had some time yet.

To spend with her.

His breathing was comfortable now, and his eyes started to stream with tears. It wasn't just the wind. He could make out formations on the ground now – someplace with hills, forests, and what looked like lakes. That was good. He'd grown up around the lake country; they had a cottage there, where they canoed and swam, and played like children in the water. The fast approach made him feel that he was coming home.

Time accelerated. He didn't.

As it turned out, time was relative. Other clichés were true too: his life did flash before him. There were some regrets – a few wasted years in his mid-twenties when he didn't do much but feel sorry for himself – but on the whole, he had good memories. Perhaps this was the meaning of heaven and hell.

Hell was living these final moments, and having to look back at a life filled with the pain he'd caused others and himself. The torments, the recriminations.

Heaven was being able to think about the sun slanting from under the clouds. Green fields dotted with buttercups. Being near the lake. Being with her, lying on a blanket after a picnic.

The ground rushed. It would be soon. It looked like he might land in one of those lakes. He waited until he was closer and changed his position so that he might fall feet first into the water, as streamlined as a loon diving for a fish. He used to jump off cliffs like this when he was a kid.

But he knew it wasn't likely he'd live. It was a last affirmation. Of his love for her.

Then he wasn't falling.

Seven things that I guarantee won't matter in 70 years

1. everything that is trending on Twitter today
2. whether you look fat in those pants
3. Facebook
4. anything you watched on TMZ
5. that big meeting with Marketing tomorrow
6. if you wrote a post on your blog today
7. your broken heart — it will be mended or decomposed by then.

Ask General Kang: Political & Economic Advice

I'd like to increase the number of surveillance cameras in my city, but I'm having trouble getting my council to agree. Any advice for a mayor with ambitions?

Surveillance cameras are a must for any would-be intergalactic overlord, which I assume is your ultimate goal. (Just as an aside, mayor is not the best platform to launch such a career, but you can manage it, particularly if you are bloodthirsty enough and have really good psycho-kinesis — the insidious Lord Bobo started as a mayor.)

Here are a few suggestions for getting your own big brother operation up-and-running:

1. Stage a series of abhorrent crimes: start small with these, and work your way up into some really nasty ultra-violence. (Think the first half-hour of *A Clockwork Orange* as a good template.) This will create your climate of fear.
2. Install cameras in high crime areas

3. Pay your goons to commit crimes in places where there are no cameras
4. Install cameras there
5. Repeat as necessary
6. Then arrest all your goons.

Now the conditions are in place for you to take the next logical step: cameras in people's houses. Look, you can argue, you've stopped violent crime and anti-social acts in the streets — imagine what you could achieve if you put cameras in people's homes? No more spouse abuse, no more child molestation. Who could be against that?

Suggest that anyone who doesn't like this plan has something to hide.

Lastly, all you need to do is start building your army. I recommend arming them with plasma weapons and hyper-kazoos. Nothing renders an enemy force more helpless (with laughter) than a phalanx of über-chimps blowing hyper-kazoos. (Then plasma weapons up the wazoo!)

Apparently, only one in four people read a book last year — how can we improve that figure?

I'd start by disabling the publishing industry in some way — perhaps an elite cadre of pulp-loving squirrels armed with plasma-shredders and capable of firing book worms out of their mouths? Or perhaps you could change the tax laws so that drinks, food and visits to literary conferences can no longer be deducted.

Then I'd start a massive PR campaign that showed (with whatever scientific research we can drum up — we'll need to set up a think tank to provide some too) that reading books is actually *harmful* to your health. We should also start some kind of fake grassroots organization that can politicize the issue for us, appealing to the public's need to "save the children."

Then, I'd –

No, no, I want *more* people to read books

Why would you want that? It makes the population much easier to control if they're illiterate, you know.

I don't want the population to be easier to control!

What are you, some kind of anarchist?

Okay. So a campaign to get more people to read. Hmmm. What if you tied lotteries to book reading? Instead of picking numbers at random, you would only pick winning numbers from a pool of those who purchased tickets and correctly answered the skill-testing question, based on the book they have claimed to have read?

Either that or have some kind of compulsory reading comprehension test every year: they get three chances to answer the questions right, and if they don't, you implant some kind of mind-control device (the X-trablian Zombie Beetle is an excellent choice) that prevents them from using the TV, Internet and radio.

Or you could force them to spend their days reading through the slush piles of romance publishers.

Do you think we should ban tasers?

Yes. I believe that tasers are a barbaric technology. Not only are tasers an excruciating way to kill people, they don't have a 100 percent efficiency rating. Many taser victims actually survive! If police forces around the world are willing to give me their tasers, I will pass along the technical schematics for a number of non-lethal devices that my Excelsior-Ape-Jackboot-and-Miniskirt Paramilitary Forces have used quite effectively to subdue the great unwashed populace, if subduing is your goal.

The Amplified Kazoo:
Amplified kazoo music is brutal. I once knew a bonobo whose atonal rendition of "Don't Cry for Me Fargentina" could drop a brigade of gorilloids armed with broadswords.

Electro-accordion
While not quite as painful as the Amplified Kazoo, Electro-accordions can work as non-lethal weapons, and are especially effective means of crowd control with young hipsters. Warning: Does not work anywhere people listen to zydeco, the Paris metro, or at Irish sessions. Electro-accordions are most effective when deployed by an armada of angry über-chimps with no sense of rhythm.

Doom-worms:
On Mephitis VI, there is a kind of multi-appendaged gut worm that can emit a high-pitched whining sound, which is a combination of noise similar to a mosquito's buzz and about 100 overtired children stuffed into a mini-van. If amplified, the sound will pop the eyes out of any primate. Warning: Handle this creature with care; each appendage of the gut worm is capable of delivering a neurotoxin that causes bits of your face to fall off and necrotize rapidly into a bubbly goo that smells worse than the Stench-Beast of Vomitus XII.

And don't worry about all those tasers. I have uses for them.

Interlude

Reassuring Fictions

In times like these, you may believe that all is well. You may enjoy watching the Olympics, eating Spam, or perhaps you have many Norwegian friends.

You may have the feeling that we live in the best of all possible worlds. Given the possibilities, the vagaries of quantum mechanics, perhaps, you think to yourself, everything is right in the world.

These are reassuring fictions.

These fictions are propagated by a number of clandestine groups; these groups run the affairs of the world from hidden bunkers, boardrooms, churches, and your medulla oblongata.

But they don't include the Masons.

The Exam Question

If Bluknark the Terrible is traveling from Alpha Centauri at the speed of light, and his friend Mistkea-a-a-k-pthi is traveling at 60 degrees from the galactic elliptic at .999 of the speed of light, from Altair, how long does it take for them to meet, and how quickly will an egg fry on your forehead while you solve this problem?

Show your work for extra points and bacon.

More Impeccably Accurate History

Selected Media Fads Through the Ages

24,000-22,000 BC: chunky fertility goddess statues

10,000 BC: cave paintings (the first graffiti)

4,000 BC: ziggurat construction

3,000-1,250 BC: pyramid raising (later revived by Mesoamericans and I.M. Pei)

1,400-500 BC: writing epic fantasy that everyone takes *way* too seriously. (Revived in the 20th century.)

500 BC-450: carving naughty things out of marble

450-800: book burning

650-850: monk burning (mostly the Vikings)

1070s: really involved tapestries depicting historical events

1347: bubo appreciation ballads

1480-1700: witch burning

1500s: homoerotic sonnet writing

1600s: pirate singing

1700s: pamphleteering

1760-1762: spreading syphilis

1790s: opera

1800s: novel-writing

1900-1914: being optimistic about the future

1919-1922: cutting up pieces of paper and pulling them out of a hat, also, painting

1925: jazz music

1927: soap-based radio

1933: burning books (mostly in Germany)

1951: find-the-commie (kind of like peek-a-boo, but with Senators)

1964: screaming (usually Beatle-related)

1966: TV

1968: painting protest signs

1976: disco

1977: DIY pet rocks

1982-1988: taking odds on Reagan-related nuclear holocaust

1987-1997: making answering machine messages

1998: web sites about your cat

1999: cappuccino drinking (related to dot-com bubble)

2000-September 2001: looking forward to the future (this didn't last as long as the previous fad in this genre)

2003: Friendster

2004-2005: blogging

2006: MySpace

2007: Facebook

2008: Twitter

2009 (Jan.-Aug): talking, writing & broadcasting about Twitter in newspapers, magazines, radio, and TV

2010 (Jan.-Feb.):getting really excited about the release of the iPad

2010 (Mar.-May): trying to remember what all the fuss about the iPad was all about

2012 (Feb.-Mar.): self-publishing collections of Internet fiction.

A Short History of Groundhog Day

On February 2, it is customary in Canada and the United States to celebrate an annual tradition wherein we allow a chubby burrowing rodent to forecast the weather. This is an important ritual, but not for the reason that many people think.

Many believe this "holiday" can be traced back to an ancient pagan ritual called Imbolc, which was duly adopted by early Christians and turned into Candlemas. (This means Mass of the Candles, in which the clergy would perform ear candling on the most hairy-eared and disgusting member of each parish, in a metaphorical recreation of the time when Jesus performed the Ear Candling of Jergomethia, cleaning the aural canals of a score of waxy hermits, and curing them of their deafness.) Finally, this holiday or "holy day" was further perverted by the German-speaking population of Pennsylvania, who fused the day with European folklore and a desire to celebrate *fersommling*, a kind of Pennsylvania Dutch orgy. (Obviously, these depravities are only celebrated by the Fancy Dutch, and eschewed by the more plain sects, such as the Amish, Mennonites and Dunkards.)

However, there live amongst some of the Elders in these plain sects of the Pennsylvania Dutch — or P-Dutch, as they are known on the mean streets of Philadelphia — the truth of Groundhog Day.

Once, North America was largely ruled by these underground rodents of the family *Sciuridae*, and though they lived largely in peace with the native human populations, the arrival of the white man marked the end of their peaceful co-existence. For when the early settlers began tearing up the forests, and plowing the meadows where the groundhog, or woodchuck, lives, war between all men and the Tcuckbar (as the groundhogs call their own race) began.

Amongst the Elders of the Dunkards, this is known as

the *Grundschwein Zehekriege*, or literally, "groundhog toe wars"; this name is taken from the favourite martial tactic of the Tcuckbar, which is to sever the large toe of a human being, and thus cause him to lose his balance and fall down, making his carotid artery available for a thorough savaging. Normally, groundhogs are peaceful herbivores, but when roused, they can eat up to twice their own weight in human flesh. (This is a little-known fact.)

It is when they are thus engorged, looking almost like a bristly boar that they are most dangerous. Indeed, one of their other names is taken from this state: while in boar mode, the average groundhog will make a high-pitched sound, from whence their nickname, "whistle pig" derives.

During this dark period of the war, many humans took to fighting one another, or slaughtering local wolf populations, for no one could believe such excessive butchery could be done by the lowly woodchuck — and the groundhog attackers were always disappearing into holes or climbing trees before humans could spot them. (You didn't know they could climb trees, did you? Then you probably also don't know about their limited psychokinetic ability to move small objects such as golf balls, musket balls, and testicles.)

Eventually, through an uncharacteristic adoption of empiric method the P-Dutch *Fußführer* (or "Foot Leader"), Johann Suppetrinker, figured out it was the groundhogs, and the war turned to the favour of the human forces. Unfortunately, most humans outside the P-Dutch Confederacy did not believe Suppetrinker's explanation, and it took many years for the humans to gain control of the situation.

To this day, crack forces of Amish and Mennonite *Grundschweinmörders* (Groundhog Killers) spend part of every winter season hunting down resistant forces of the dangerous Tcuckbar groundhog clans. Luckily, evolution has done the rest of the work for us, and the remaining non-sentient species is largely harmless, except to the occasional horse or golfer.

But this is why we celebrate Groundhog Day with an

annual humiliation ritual. What other possible explanation could there be for the pomp and elaborate circumstance of this winter rite? Punxsutawney Phil and Wiarton Willie are not terrified by their own shadow, so much as each of them are experiencing a deep racial memory of seeing the figure of an Amish *Grundschweinmörder*, poised to spit them on a finely crafted *spitzerstock*. (Pointed stick.)

And they've only been slightly more accurate at predicting the end of winter than the Farmer's Almanac, the P-Dutch edition included.

Forgotten Deities: Flaccidus, The Roman God of Engineers

Flaccidus was a god revered during the time of the Roman Republic.

Flaccidus was a kind of angry god, but not in the Mars I'm-going-to-stab-you-with-a-spear way, but in a passive aggressive, I'm-going-to-make-your-spear-limp, kind of way. For example, if you had something that required stiffness, and *Flaccidus* didn't look favourably on you, then the object you would very much like to stay upright would droop at inopportune times.

Most engineers in the Roman construction industry were active worshippers of *Flaccidus*, and they would sacrifice to him weekly, because — let's face it — there's nothing worse than having one of your erections fall flat. Not to mention the dangers of sinking bridges, droopy apartment buildings, and aqueducts that can't keep it up. Naturally, our English word, flaccid, comes from this Latin root.

Interestingly, worship of *Flaccidus* waned in the early part of the Roman Empire, when a mystery cult devoted to a blue-faced Eastern god named *Via Gara* became quite popular.

Favourite form of sacrifice: a male chicken, still in the state of *rigor mortis*. The Romans thought that would work for some reason.

As a Canadian, I'm politely outraged by all the misconceptions people from other countries have about our history and culture. I hope this list clears everything up.

Ten indisputable facts about Canada

One: The Vikings

The first Europeans to arrive in Canada were the Vikings, in 1009, more than 1000 years ago. Their leader, Leif The Abrasive, was told by several Irish monks they had visions of a "vast and rich land" that lay across the Atlantic Ocean. Leif, who was torturing them at the time, took them at their word and immediately launched a massive invasion. Many of the longboats sank in the crossing, but the core band arrived in Newfoundland (which the Vikings optimistically called "Vinland", as they expected to find many fine wines in this new world — a hope which would not be fulfilled until the early 1990s.) Initially, the Viking settlement was successful, winning several Juno Awards — a kind of Canadian Grammy — but soon they split because of "creative differences". Little was heard of them afterwards, but one of the members later had an interesting show about the early days of Viking rock on CBC Radio.

Two: Other Invasions

The next massive invasion came from the French, who had an insatiable thirst for beaver. Eventually, the British invaded too, declaring that they also had a hunger for "beaver and other pelts", but really they were just jealous of the French, who were so good at trapping and mating with the cute, industrious rodents. Throughout this period, the aboriginal populations of Canada (erroneously called "Indians" because of the navigationally challenged racist Christopher Columbus), tried to cope with their perverted new neighbors, though they never understood them.

Three: Canada does not mean "village"

Many people believe the name Canada is based on the Iroquois word "kanata" or "village." The sad truth is Canada is named after Lord Alfred O. Canada, the first Twit Plenipotentiary sent by the British Crown to rule over the beaver-addled country with an iron fist (he'd lost his original hand in the Battle of Ipswich — fought between the Dutch, the French and the British over who was going to pick up the cheque at the annual Let's Rape the New World Convention and BeaverFest) and his laser-beam-firing eyes. (He is an ancestor of Queen Victoria.) Though he was a twit, Lord Alfred's powerful eyes were capable of levelling cities, and the primitive flintlocks used at the time could not penetrate the force shield he was able to generate with the power of his idiocy. He fed himself on a steady diet of French babies and British virgins (who were plentiful in the Age of the Pox). Many Canadians were lost in the battle against the depredations of Lord Alfred, but eventually, he was tricked into getting into a canoe just upriver of Niagara Falls. (The clever rebel force had placed a sign on the canoe that said, "Fresh French baby here"). When he was in the canoe, confused by the lack of baby, the plucky freedom fighters pushed the craft into the swift current. The heroic rebels were vaporized by Lord Alfred's fiery gaze as he went over the falls, but their plan had succeeded: the Twit Plenipotentiary fell to his death as not even his incredibly stupidity field could save him.

Niagara Falls is a venerated site because of this history, and most Canadians will, at some point, make the pilgrimage to Niagara Falls where they gaze respectfully at the power of the natural wonder for at least five minutes. They will then spend the afternoon looking at freaks.

Canadians decided to take the name that had been such a trial, and use it to remind themselves of their resilience and fortitude. Furthermore, early Canadians immortalized this story by turning it into Canada's national anthem:

> O. Canada,
> You evil, nasty man,
> Never again will babies be e-a-ten!
> With glowing hearts we see thee fall
> Thy hand of iron a weight.
> From far and wide, O. Canada
> With you we're quite irate.
> God keep our land, British twit free!
> O. Canada we stand on guard from thee.
> O. Canada we stand on guard from thee.

Four: The National Capital Region

Despite the victory over Lord Alfred O. Canada, the British Crown continued to make decisions for the peoples of Canada — they just stopped sending the twits here, and made their determinations in the UK; this is why the capital of the country is in Ottawa. Sitting on the south bank of the Ottawa River, the city is the fourth-coldest capital within parsecs. The only colder capitals are Ulaanbaatar (Mongolia), Moscow (Russia) and Pakit! (Hoth). What many people do not realize is that it is also: a) one of the most humid capitals in the world (in the months of June-August) and b) the center of an underground civilization populated by Morlocks.

The Morlocks, as you know, see human beings as a food source, but they are quite conservative in their culling practices, which incorporate a model of sustainability and eugenics many economists describe as "exemplary". The Morlocks have found that it is most efficient to eat only the most intelligent males in the National Capital Region. This explains the predominance of women in the civil service (one of Ottawa's major industries). One supposes the Morlocks do not cull the intelligent females, because they are confident that the remaining male population will be of little interest to the women. In fact, Queen Victoria's twits actually knew about this, which is why they built Canada's parliament in this region, ensuring the safety of Canada's politicians for generations to come. (At this point in history, the British still held out hopes that they might return to Canada and rule in person.) **Note**: Many textbooks will tell you that Ottawa was not made the capital until 1867, but this is, in fact, a persistent and malicious typo. It was 1847.

Five: The BNA Act

Despite their alleged abhorrence of violence, Canadians have traditionally been fierce warriors. During the War of 1812, for example, Canada was defended from US invaders not by the British Army, nor our own irregular troops (they were all engaged in a real war with Napoleon Bonaparte), but by a cadre of little schoolgirls and one-legged lumberjacks. (Thus explaining the draw, or if you're an American student of history, the "victory".) No Canadian warrior was more fierce than the Scottish-born firebrand John Alexander "The Madman" Macdonald. He rose to prominence during the first Zombie War, 1837, and was elected to Parliament. (It is worth noting that The Madman is one of the few intelligent politicians to survive Morlock culling practices; while he was still young and hale, The Madman would spend many an evening in the underground world, doing a little culling of his own. He led a group of Morlock-hunters called the Association of Really Ripped Gentlemen (ARRG) in his off-hours.)

As he aged, The Madman discovered that he was able to feign stupidity by keeping himself "well-medicated" with scotch. Despite this impediment, he was still able to convince the British crown to allow Canada to govern itself, forming a "Confederation" under the Beaver Not Actually needed Act (BNA Act). This piece of legislation forms, essentially, the constitution of Canada. After achieving Confederation, Macdonald went on to enlist the help of the Association of

Really Ripped Gentlemen (ARRG) in building a railroad across Canada, eliminate all the vampires from the Northwest Territories, and invent the game of hockey.

Six: Hockey

If you are familiar with Canada, you may have heard something about hockey — or ice hockey, as it is known in countries where other, sissified forms of hockey are more popular. Hockey is quite possibly the most important thing in Canadian culture. Did you know that most Canadians emerge from the womb clutching a tiny hockey stick? Did you also know that infants who do not have a hockey stick when they are born are given one by the National Hockey Commission? It's true. (Though quite often the Canadian babies born without hockey sticks must have it duct-taped to their tiny fists.) Hockey was invented by Canada's first Prime Minister, John A. "The Madman" Macdonald and his Association of Really Ripped Gentlemen (ARRG) in 1847 (the same year the Canadian parliament was built in Ottawa). Hockey permeates Canadian society the way that guns permeate US culture. When there is no ice to play on, Canadians make do with roads, sidewalks and abandoned tennis courts to play their favourite game. There are probably about 29-million people playing hockey right now in Canada. (The other four million are either too infirm or too drunk to play, or they are part of the small percentage of selfless Canadians who keep our various hockey-supporting infrastructures serviced, including the universal hockey injury health service, the power grid that lights Canadian hockey rinks, and of course, the lumberjacks who chop down the trees we use in the creation of hockey sticks.)

Seven: Timmys

Almost as important as hockey, Timmys, or Tim Hortons, is Canada's national coffee chain. (It may be no surprise to learn that Tim Horton was a legendary hockey star, capable of decapitating his opponents with one slash of his razor-sharp hockey stick.) Timmys is best known for its highly addictive coffee, made from the distilled sweat of NHL hockey players, ultra-caffeine, *phenylcyclohexylpiperidine* (PCP), and one supposes some form of coffee bean, though the dark coloring may be provided by some kind of cocaine-based food dye. Timmys coffee is powerful enough to wake even a thoroughly hung-over hockey dad at 4 am, as he attempts to deliver his hockey-addled progeny to a 5 am practice.

Eight: International Stars

You may not realize this, but one of Canada's major exports is international stars. In fact, fully 63.2% of our Gross National Product is the result of remittances from our international stars. What stars am I talking about? Well, the Department of International Entertainer Breeding has been most successful at creating three kinds of super stars:

- **female singers** Celine Dion, Joni Mitchell, Avril Lavigne, Alanis Morrisette, Shania Twain, Justin Bieber, etc.
- **comics**: Dan Aykroyd, Mike Myers, Jim Carrey, Howie Mandel, Lorne Michaels, most of Second City, the Kids in the Hall, etc.
- **actors**: Michael J Fox, Kiefer Sutherland, Keanu Reeves, Ryan Gosling, Ryan Reynolds, Rachel McAdams, Seth Rogan, etc.

I would like to take this opportunity to apologize for this to our good American neighbours, but really, what choice do we have? We would go broke without them. Though we really are very, very sorry about Celine. It's really generous of the US to store her in Vegas for us.

Nine: The CBC

Many of you may have heard of the Canadian Broadcasting Corporation, which is purportedly Canada's national broadcaster, running services in both English and French; the CBC has television and radio stations across the country. This, is, of course, a front.

In fact, the CBC is a highly trained cadre of scientists, weapon-specialists, and blade-wielding warriors who keep Canada safe from the next outbreak of zombies. (This is always a danger, particularly in the summer months after the NHL hockey season is over, when Canadian men, in particular, are prone to fits of zombie-ism.)

Without the brave and tireless work of the CBC, Canada would have long been overrun by zombies. Even so, some taxpayers think it would be nice not to have to pay for CBC TV.

Ten: William Shatner

William Shatner is a treasure in both Canada *and* the US, so he gets his own category.

It is just a matter of time until we have a National Holiday named after him. (Personally, I think we should have some kind of break in March, perhaps coinciding with his birthday.)

Regina Atroxica: A list

1. Queen Victoria was born of German descent: her father was Prince "Schnitzel" Edward, Duke of Kent and Strathearn and her mother was a stein of Pilsner.

2. If Victoria had been under 18 when the King died, then her mother would have acted as regent, provided the Household Guard could prevent her being quaffed by thirsty staff.

3. Victoria was the first Queen of England who had the ability to fire laser beams from her eyes.

4. She was the first reigning monarch to live in Buckingham Palace, which was paid for entirely by taxing the consumption of expertly-cooked meals. (Thus explaining generations of atrocious food in the UK.)

5. Her mother's brother (uncle) was King Leopold I of Belgium; he spent most days attempting to drink his sister.

6. Her husband, Prince Albert of Saxe-Coburg and Gotha, could not speak a word of English and was her cousin.

7. Most people are surprised to learn that Victoria had the ability to speak through her genitals. Her favourite genitals were, in order: Lord Melbourne, Lord Beaconsfield and Lord Salisbury.

8. Her husband died of typhus, contracted because of the primitive sanitary conditions at Windsor Castle, and because he did not believe in "washing, *per se*".

9. Distraught after the death of her husband, Victoria went on a world-wide rampage, incinerating all who resisted her, founding Canada, New Zealand, and conquering the lands of Ireland, Scotland and India. After this, colonists called her *Regina Atroxica*, or Horrible Queen.

10. Before dying, she uttered the famous, but often misquoted phrase: "If you do not worship me henceforth, I shall not be amused, and my revenant will consume your children and beer as you wail in agony as I cook you where you stand."

Ask General Kang: The Home World

What is the penalty for plagiarism on your planet?

Plagiarism is the "act of stealing the ideas and/or expressions of another and representing them as your own," though I can't remember where I got that quote from — just Google it for the source.

On my home planet of Neecknaw, this is not only an academic offence, but it is also a capital crime.

This stems from the days of Kargnak the Betrayed, one of the great warlord monkey rulers of the ancient days. Legend has it that Kargnak was an impressionable young screen-writer before he became the first in a long line of bloodthirsty intergalactic conquerors from the Planet Neecknaw.

As it happens, he wrote a promising screenplay called, "Planet of the Hairless Hominids", about a dystopic future in which all good Neecknabian chimps were ruled by self-absorbed, ecologically retarded hominids he styled "humans". (We had yet to discover the Milky Way Galaxy and your backwards corner of it in those days.) A producer showed some interest in it, but alas, did not buy the manuscript.

And wasn't Kargnak surprised when the next summer, "Planet of the Humans" appeared at his local Chimpaplex? It was a huge hit, and made millions, and was (of course) based entirely on Kargnak's original screenplay. He didn't see a single banana skin for it, and thus Kargnak gave up the writing game for the bloodthirsty and cruel warlord business. At which he was moderately successful, taking over all of Neecknaw and some of our neighboring planets. (After levelling the Neecknabian movie industry.)

Actually, he didn't give up writing completely, as he penned the Kargnakian Code, which for the first time set out all of our laws in a logical and ordered way. Under the Kargnakian Code, plagiarism is a capital crime, and the condemned are put to death by having all their hairs plucked out (very painful when you're covered with hair), then having a thousand unpublished writers slicing the plagiarist with the sharpest paper they can find, while lemons are crushed in a massive press above them, weighed down by the manuscripts of a thousand unpublished writers. Oh, and hot pokers are inserted wherever paper cuts cannot be administered.

Good god, that's horrible! What about self-plagiarism?

Self-plagiarism is style, baby.

What do you do when your planet runs out of resources?

What do I do? Shouldn't you be asking what will you do?

What *I* do is charge up the power cells in my Interstellar Ape-arda, fill the ships with hordes of über-chimps hungry for adventure and loot, and set course for the nearest planet that hasn't used up all its resources.

From there, it's a simple matter of subduing the local sapient population (if there is one), and then setting up shop. Literally. The second major phase of any decent conquest is building the consumer infrastructure you need to plunder a planet. You'd be amazed how many societies are content to live within their means. Sustainable development is no good if you're in the pillaging business!

But that's what *I'd* do (if I still had a fleet of space ships capable of faster-than-light travel and crammed full of bonobos with a jones for gold-plated walking sticks).

You can barely reach your own planet's orbit, so *you're* going to have to come up with a more creative solution.

Do you celebrate Thanksgiving on your home world?

No, we have several holidays that are somewhat similar, but essentially we break your celebration into two components. And then we have one "thanksgiving" day which is totally alien to your world.

In the late months of the harvest time on Planet Neecknaw, we have a holiday that is probably closest to your Thanksgiving (which is really just a North American holiday, not a global phenomenon, by the way.)

Cram It!

Our harvest festival is called Cram It! The name really explains it all. The focus is on the cramming or stuffing of things: delicate fruits and nuts into the hollowed-out abdominal cavities of tasty and unsuspecting fowl; this and other foods crammed into the gullets of a glutinous simian horde; and for those monkeys who haven't overdone the gastronomical cramming, there is a special "evening" cramming that happens when the little macaques are in bed, if you get my drift.

Famanguish

We then let the hangover from our Saturnalia-like Cram It! become a distant memory, before we celebrate Famanguish Day, which is when we force ourselves to spend the day with our extended family (whom we usually never see) and ask them to revive all of our crippling emotional traumas. Some families are more creative and come up with new traumas especially for that day. Sometimes many. Nobody looks forward to Famanguish, but everyone participates because, "you only have one family."

Kangsgiving

Then when I was Overlord, I instituted Kangsgiving Day, which followed the day after Famanguish. Kangsgiving is a day of rest, during which you are supposed to sit at home and quietly thank me for not forcing you to go to work after the horrors of Famanguish. Also, you can drink as much coconut or banana liqueur as you'd like, as long as you agree to do a tour of duty in my crack Gorilloid Toilet Cleaning Service. This is a non-combat unit whose sole duty is to clean up after the Gorilloid Army. They can be messy — oh, let's not mince words, the Gorilloid Army makes the Savage Poo-Flinging Brigade look fastidious — but hey, all the banana liqueur you want … and I send it to your house.

Fabulist Satire, Redux

Those Pernicious Business Clichés

Tolbert Whistlebaum had a deep and abiding love for the English language, which is why he took a doctorate at Oxford University, concentrating on Naughty Victorian Literature.

His scholarship was insufficient to cover his tuition and his love affair with first edition copies of Richard Burton's translation of the Kama Sutra (eventually they became unreadable), so he took on a copy-editing job with the marketing division of Gargantuan Enterprises. His boss was a lovely and exciting woman, but she did nothing to stop the linguistic excrescences that his co-workers produced on a daily basis, such as turning nouns into verbs, using buzz words to the point of incomprehensibility and generally, being "proactive".

Eventually, Whistlebaum couldn't take it anymore and he did a little "rightsizing" at the company through a new "aggressive interface paradigm".

The survivors later agreed that his presentation had been quite "impactful".

The All-Gas Mask Revival of Hamlet

The 1937 all-gas mask revival of Hamlet at the Birmingham Repertory Theatre would have probably gone down in the annals of theatre history as the best all-gas mask production — of any play — if the director, Sir Albert Fezbinder had not insisted on actually gassing the audience after Hamlet uttered his final line, "the rest is silence."

By all surviving accounts, a young Laurence Olivier was riveting as the famed Prince of Denmark. One critic, Thesper Citrus-Fruit, managed to drag himself from the theatre, leaving a trail of bits of lung behind him, and penned a short critical haiku before expiring:

>Olivier brill!
>His eyes pierce even rubber
>Mustard triumphant.

Blogger Ponders on Things Instead of Musing About Them

LONDON, ONTARIO (The Skwib) — The web is still reeling from the revelation that a blogger has been pondering things instead of musing about them.

"Yeah, I've spent a lot of time musing, in fact, the tagline from my blog used to be 'muted musings from Jeff's tasty trumpet" — clever, eh? But . . . I don't know, it just seemed like it was time to, you know, start pondering instead," Jeffrey Trumpeter told The Skwib in an early morning phone interview.

Trumpeter runs Assorted Cream Fillings (pudding-like ponderings from Jeffrey's pastry pan), a blog devoted to his interest in cats, Boston Cream Donuts, hockey, politics and humor he describes as either "quirky" or "explosive".

"Yeah, I'm pretty happy with the change in direction. I think I'll keep pondering on things for a while," Trumpeter said.

According to experts, Trumpeter is one of many bloggers who are shifting their mode of cogitation.

"We have been tracking this development with new blogging software, ThoughtCounter, and we may be reaching the tipping point away from musing," Leslie Flapkake, PhD candidate at a "leading university", told The Skwib.

"Musings are still the most popular form of cogitation," Flapkake said, "but you see people pondering, reflecting, mulling, brooding and even thinking."

The chart that follows is courtesy of ThoughtCounter:

Varieties of cogitation used on blogs

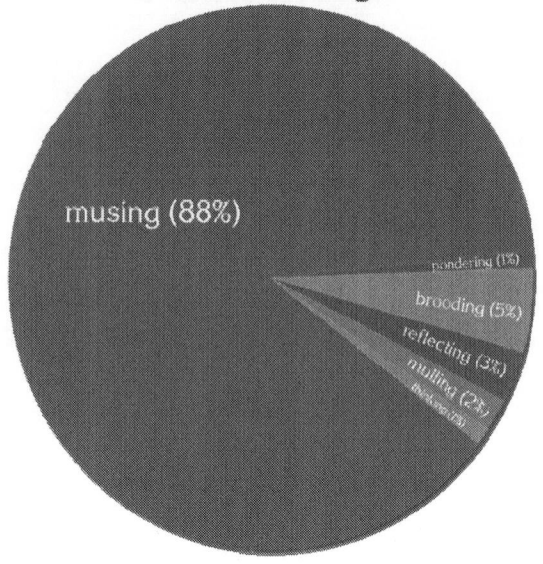

- musing (88%)
- pondering (1%)
- brooding (5%)
- reflecting (3%)
- mulling (2%)
- ruminating (1%)

Leda and the Swan

Naturally, Zeus was attracted to Leda, but what was the best way to get her attention? Should he appear as a shower of gold, or as a gigantic human hurling lightning bolts? Perhaps just hurl gold? That should get any woman's attention, surely?

Maybe he should just take a straightforward approach, and introduce himself. Take a risk and just say, "Hey, Leda, you know, I think you're kind of a swell person and I think we should get to know one another."

Or maybe something more risqué like: "Leda, I think you're a beautiful woman, and I'd like to buy you a steak."

Or, he could take the form of a swan and "stick her with the bill."

William Shatner's Inaugural Address (After Winning the First Post-Two-Party Presidential Election)

Friends, Americans, Countrymen! Lend me your ears. I come to bury our two-party system, not praise it. I stand before you today, not as a conqueror, not as pop icon, but as your President. An American president.

Many of you are worried about my Canadian birth, but I would like to assure you that I am an American through and through — I have been for many years.

I bet you few, pathetic, angry, *angry*, Republicans left standing now regret amending the Constitution so the Governator could be eligible, don't you? Eh? Just a little bit?

Come on, a robot against Captain Kirk? It's insulting!

Our new system will have to adapt, to find new worlds, to boldly go where no POTUS has gone before. I gotta tell you, this is more fun than pantsing George Takei. (Though I think he secretly enjoyed it.) They told me to be Presidential, so I should say that I intend to bring our country together. No more petty infighting between two groups that represent the same interests. Instead, we can look forward to petty infighting among dozens of groups, which represent the same interests.

My party, the Federation Party (or the Star Trek Party as it's known to the Twitterati) is open to all Americans. It is a cooperative party, which is why WE are forming a government. If we can cooperate with the Star Wars Ascendancy Party of America and the American Stargate Association, then we can cooperate with anyone. Even Ralph Nader.

I'm looking forward to working with my Vice-President, Mark Hamill. He looks easy to control. I like that. I'm not sure about Richard Dean Anderson. The agreement is that we'll make him the Secretary of State, but I'm not sure he's up to it. I think we should give him Transportation or Energy where he can do less damage, but the agreement was State, so what the hell.

Since this is my inaugural address, I should give you some kind of indication of where I plan to take the country in the next four years. Space, naturally. If I don't do something space-wise the fanboys are going to crucify me. Seriously, the only reason I'm not wearing a Starfleet uniform to this inauguration thing is that I threatened to turn everything over to Hamill if they made me wear it.

So Mars, definitely. And whatever new gizmos we can come up with. Personally, I want a phaser that will allow me to stun Leonard Nimoy's cryogenically preserved head whenever he starts to go on a policy rant. He helped me run a great campaign and he's gonna be a terrifying Chief of Staff: you should see the robot chassis we've got for the head.

Now, are there any Democrats here today? No? I know there are quite a few left — pun intended! I doubt they're going to be viable much longer, though. The Oprah Party is pretty much taking over what's left of their base, and my guess is she'll be tough in the next election.

But today is all about me! And America. Yay, America!

For all you Canadians secretly gleeful about my election as the President of the United States, I have some good news. We're going to look at ways to make it a bit easier for you to work here. However, we'll need to annex most of the provinces and territories, though I don't think we'll want Manitoba. Have any of you ever been at Portage and Main in February? Forget about it!

Now, let's go crack open some beers, and get down. Later, I'll be joining the band and we'll do a few numbers from my new album.

Finally, something in politics that we can all look forward to!

The Gruntwerx Paradigm

Gunter was employed by the spectacularly successful IT consulting company, Gruntwerx.

Why was Gruntwerx the acme of the German IT world? Because they didn't whine. They didn't complain about anything. Complaining caused negative energy, wasted time, and brought everyone down, the CEO of Gruntwerx, Helga von Werthog, said.

"Two moans and you're out," she said. And she meant it. It was in all their employment contracts. Half of their analysts had been fired for whining on the job.

It was hard to argue with their success. Even with the downturn in the economy, revenue and profits were way up. But the strain was starting to show.

"Good morning, Gunter," his manager Bernhard Dink said as Gunter walked into the office, a bit late. "You're tardy."

"Are you complaining about it?" Gunter asked.

"No, just noting the fact."

"Ah. My apologies. My train was delayed."

"And…"

"And that's okay!" Gunter enthused. He smiled as broadly as he could. Of course, he wanted to scream: "and it sucks! I get in trouble because the bloody train is late!" But he did not. He was a happy, productive worker. He had a job.

He also had an ulcer, and a throbbing vein in his temple that was worrying. His co-workers dealt with the stress in other ways. Werner had taken up karate and self-flagellation. Hedrick was on a cocktail of mood-altering drugs that kept him happy, sedate, and incapable of enjoying marital relations with his leggy wife, Lisle.

Gunter had been looking for employment elsewhere, someplace where he could speak his mind on occasion. But it

pirate therapy ○ 139

was a shrinking market, not to mention that more and more companies, particularly in the IT industry, had taken up the Gruntwerx paradigm.

The only thing keeping him sane was his hobby, taxidermy, and the self-help group that had formed from the most disgruntled Gruntwerx employees — they met secretly once a week for what they called sessions of "über-bitch".

He would survive it. He'd survived countless other management fads: TQM, quality circles, excellence, matrix management, and on, and on. He would survive the Gruntwerx paradigm too. He sat down at his desk and began the work day, content with the knowledge that he would rise above von Werthog and her corporate censorship.

There was a hubbub in the common area, where a TV usually displayed the news. His co-workers looked worried, as they watched. It was their Chancellor, announcing a new sweeping law based on the Gruntwerx paradigm.

"If Germany is going to weather this global economic crisis, we must change the way we think. We must be positive. From this day forward, the German people are not allowed to complain, whine, whinge or moan about things, under penalty of law," he said.

"Isn't it wonderful?" Bernhard Dink asked the assembled Gruntwerx employees.

"Oh . . . uh, yes, yes," they all muttered, but not Gunter.

He was already back in his office, calling an old army buddy, who dealt in illegal arms.

Daisy of Narnia Reveals the Ugly Truth

'Allo, dearie, I suppose you'd like to hear all about your hero Aslan and those Pevensie folk, but you don't want to hear it from the likes of me.

You want to talk to Edmund's horse Phillip or p'raps those Beavers (desperate suck-ups the Beavers). They'll tell you what you want to hear.

Now, don't get me wrong. I was not a fan of that bitch queen at all. Not at all. Us Jersey cows are not made for the cold, and the White Witch had the thermostat turned down all the time, but at least when she was running things, me and the other ladies were more or less left to our own devices.

But since the Pevensies have taken over the establishment, it has been nothing but toil for the likes of me. I get milked at least once a day, usually by that pervert Mr. Tumnus.

(Would it surprise you know that he always has a slurp of me longer teat before he milks t'others? He bites a bit too.)

And don't get me started on General Otmin. You'd think a famous centaur like that would have his choice of lady centaurs, and even horses, 'fer Christ's sake, but he has a taste for the Jersey, if you get me meanin'.

But it's not so much the milking and unwanted attention. It's what happens to the young 'uns, the male young 'uns.

It's not like that Christmas roast just magically appears, you see.

Dr. Tundra Versus the Flashmob Zombies

Dr. Maximilian Tundra had never felt so paranoid.

Earlier that day he'd lost his medical licence; luckily, he also had a PhD in biochemistry, so he could still get everyone to call him "doctor". But it was the loss of easy access to pharmaceuticals that was the problem.

No, he had to be honest with himself: the problem was the special Halloween pumpkin-and-peyote-extract milkshake he'd had at breakfast, a couple hours before the hearing.

Four hours later the anxiety and fear were at their highest. He knew that, but of course, he didn't have complete control over it.

Then he saw the zombies.

Serious, honest-to-god zombies. They filled the street. A small group of brain-hungry shufflers were chasing patrons out of an Aldo store and biting them. There was a zombie staring right at Dr. Tundra. It looked like he used to be a priest and was finishing off an afternoon snack of tasty baby.

The screams were horrible, terrifying. Already unhinged by his de-licencing and the ill-advised peyote pick-me-up, Dr. Tundra started to shake. If he'd had more control over his body, Tundra would have run, but he didn't.

What he did have was his .45. And enough practice that he was confident the fear and mescaline would not ruin his aim.

"Shoot for the head," he reminded himself, as he approached the mob of zombies. Many of them seemed to be laughing and having a good time. He thought that was odd. Zombies shouldn't laugh.

And he certainly didn't expect them to run away.

A Reluctant Emcee

The stun bolt struck near me, and I was flying through the air. My hair crackled with static electricity. My vision went red. Quite possibly I soiled my expensive trousers. Did any of that worry me? No, I had much bigger problems. My brothers were coming back to town for the wedding.

I'd been dreading both events. Their inevitable return, and the marriage of Josh and Mary. Just as inevitable: the lovebirds' request to have me, the Right Honorable Member of Parliament for Middlesex County, Ab Durer, as master of ceremonies.

I loathe the role of emcee. And my friends *always* ask me to do it.

Earlier that week, I'd foolishly complained to my brother Warren about emceeing again; he'd looked particularly scary in a suit of plate mail he always "wore" in the datasphere. An affectation, but it had plenty of impact.

"Well, why don't me and the other brothers come?" he'd said.

"Uh. I'm not sure how good an idea that is," I had said.

"Sure! It's been ages since we saw you. Fabian and Petrovich have been pretty busy in Central America, but me and Deeter can convince them to come up."

"No, I really don't think you should. You're not invited."

"Hey!" shouted Warren, "we're never invited. Just suck it up. We're going to be there. Besides, Albrecht," he said — emphasizing the "brecht", just the way I've always hated it — "we have something to tell you."

It had taken me a while to work up the courage to let Josh and Mary know that all four were planning to attend. Mary had burst into tears, and Josh confided, "You know, I thought this relationship was just going to be the end of my bachelorhood, not the end of everything."

I'd laughed and mumbled something about the boys being much more mellow since they'd left high school. You had to admire the couple's pluck. They made contingency plans, booking a full riot squad for the reception, buying doses of the best nanobiotics money could buy, and hiring Freeze-A-Head, "in case" of fatalities.

I felt so bad that I actually gave them my speech to vet, though I figured we would never get through the wedding, let alone the speeches. I was kind of torn on that. I hate emceeing — blathering into a holo-mic so that the relatives and friends attending remotely can enjoy the syrupy sentiments. And while everyone else whiffs up jazzy nanocaines and quaffs copious amounts of Old Nurberg's Pink Ale (*those who like it like it enough to go blind*), I have to abstain.

On the other hand, did I really want to see my brothers back in town, just to avoid sobriety?

But I should get back to the stun bolts, and my electric fandango as I flew through the air, shouldn't I?

ooo

News of my brothers' impending arrival had preceded them, and there was somewhat of a panic in the sedate town of London, Ontario, County Seat of Middlesex, in His Majesty's Parliamentary Democracy of America. I was out on the front steps of the Old Court House, hoping that the solid granite building would lend dignity and seriousness to my message. I was trying to allay the fears of the sensible populace of London, Ont., when a riot broke out.

It might have been something I said.

I was outlining how London, Ontario, was an important city in the PDA, and that the king was fully aware of our situation, *and* that all of our emergency services were at the highest alert. "There is virtually no problem that we are not prepared for," I'd told them. "We can handle almost any emergency, short of a full-scale nuclear attack."

Then one of those darned reporters shouted out, "Did you know that Warren's girlfriend broke up with him?"

"Oh shit!" I'd blurted out, just like my handlers were always telling me not to do.

It was a candid response. Warren can be especially murderous after a fight with his girlfriend, a data-composer known as Strife Missouri. In the datasphere his plate mail is all show, but it speaks to Warren's underlying character. Or lack thereof.

Anyway, my uncensored fear ruptured the calm of the crowd, and the next thing I knew, the police were unleashing stun cannons on the guests, the reporters, municipal officials, and worst of all, me. I remember thinking — as I flew through the air and started to lose consciousness — *well, at least I won't be awake when my brothers ride into town.*

ooo

But I was wrong on that as well. They'd been held up in Kansas, on their way northward from the Skinny States of Central America; a series of tornadoes had destroyed the state's water purification plants and led to an outbreak of mega-cholera. Petrovich was in his effluvial element there, and they decided to "hang out," as they called it, and watch him do his thing for a while.

They stayed out of trouble as they rode through the rest of the Kingdom of the United States, and they didn't do anything until they crossed the St. Clair River and the border, in Windsor. Deeter and Fabian were pretty well behaved, but Petrovich and Warren went on a serious tear. It will take years for the strip clubs in Windsor to recover. Warren went postmodern postal on the Badlaw gang that ran "The Peekaboo", one of the city's seedier joints. While he took the place apart, he claimed that he was part of the rival gang, the Heaven's Devils, who ran the "Bustier Barn" across town. By the end of the evening, a full-scale gang war was on; car bombs were going off, there were machine-gun firefights, and Warren was happy as a Texas governor *not* commuting a death sentence. Petrovich had ensconced himself in the cathouse and proceeded to infect everyone there with a nasty strain of *genitebola*. Between the two of them, they devastated the red light district and all of its customers.

Windsor was never going to be the same, and London was trembling at their approach. Warren had stolen a number of X-Harleys from the Badlaws, and convinced our brethren to eschew their more traditional mode of transport for the sporty fuel-cell "extreme" cycles. They roared along the ancient, cracked pavement on old Highway 401.

When I came to, an apoplectic Mayor told me the news.

"Isn't there anything you can do?" she asked, her normally coiffed hair disheveled and — to be frank — kind of sexy. Catastrophe suited the Mayor.

"Your Honor," I croaked (stun cannons are notorious for drying out the soft tissues), "I have no more control over them than the wind, or the stars."

"Oh God," the Mayor moaned most attractively. "And we just opened the new convention center. Do you think they'll go there?"

"Probably not. We've moved the wedding to a horse farm north of town."

"Oh, that's a relief," the Mayor said.

"Unless you've been advertising the new convention center on the datasphere. Deeter is quite the tourist, and he'll want to see it if you have."

"But we had to tell people about it," the Mayor wailed. Not as attractive.

"Don't worry, Your Honour, I will try to appeal to their hometown pride. Now, where are my clothes?"

"Hmm. I'm afraid the trousers had to be incinerated," the Mayor said. "One of your parliamentary assistants was good enough to bring some sweats in, though."

That didn't bode well. When it came to my brothers, I needed to feel as confident as possible, and sweatpants were not going to do it.

So I took the time to go home and change into my riding leathers, and I got Betsy out of the barn. As I'd promised the lovely Mayor, I rode out on horseback to meet the boys on the outskirts of town. I hoped to change their minds.

They soon appeared in a cloud of dust. Warren led as he always did. He put up his hand, and the others brought their X-Harleys to a muttering stop. Weeds grew in the ancient asphalt, sticking up between the spokes of their wheels. It was a hot early July day, just before "Canada Day" as we still subversively dubbed the July 4th weekend in the Parliamentary Democracy of America.

"Ab!" Fabian said. "You're a sight for hungry eyes. I never thought I'd see you on the back of a horse again, let alone on old Betsy."

"Yeah, well, it seemed like the right occasion."

"So is this going to be a great party, or what? Aaaaaalbrecht?" Warren asked. He wore a menacing look, shadowed underneath the old German helmet he'd taken off of some Windsor Badlaw he'd trounced the night before.

"I know why you're here, Ab," Deeter jumped in before anyone else spoke. As much as Warren liked to think of himself as their leader, Deeter was the oldest and their final arbiter. "You're here to ask us not to come into town. This town. Where we were born."

"Well," I said, hoping to sound reasonable, "yes. Didn't you like London?"

"Of course," said Deeter, smiling, remembering the carnage of his high school prom. "Good times. But that has nothing to do with it."

"It doesn't?"

"No. You see, Ab, the wedding was just an excuse for our visit. We just don't have the leeway to overlook someone who's not committed to the family business."

I was suddenly alarmed. Until that moment, I'd never seen them as a threat to me, so much as a threat to the rest of the world. Still, something prompted me to ask: "Why not?"

"Well, our work is unambiguous. You're a little too … diplomatic. This whole emcee business, for instance. You don't like to do it, but you keep saying yes. Why?"

"Well, it's an honor to be asked, but more than that … I know I can do a good job."

"But it doesn't really fit with the family, does it? We need some help. Otherwise, you know we might have to cut you off."

I really didn't like the sound of that. It sounded like something Warren might take literally. "Cut me off?"

"Yeah. We need some help. Direction. Structure. Some stories or jokes to explain what we're doing. At first, I was really excited that you chose politics. What a great, modern way to bring about the end."

"It's always been important in my line," Warren growled approvingly.

"But now," Deeter said, "I'm not sure that politics is exactly right. Maybe media would be better. Anyway, we're sure you'll come up with the right solution. We'll give you some time to think about it, and don't worry, we're not really going to the wedding. We're off to the Middle East."

"The Middle East again?"

"Looove the classics," shouted Warren. Maniac.

"Remember, little brother," said Deeter as they rode away, "we need your help. We'll cut you off if we have to, but we'd rather see you…." His last words were drowned out in the roar of the X-Harleys, and I sat there on Betsy, feeling chilled despite the heat.

148 ○ mark a. rayner

They wanted me to be *their* emcee too.

I turned Betsy around, and she trotted home faithfully. Betsy was a lovely, gentle bay, who'd never done anything wrong in her whole life. She just seemed so happy as we walked along the weed-choked remains of the 401. It was weird to think that I might have to ride her for real.

I got back to London; its people heaved a collective sigh of relief when they found out my brothers were headed elsewhere. Before the ceremony I worked a bit more on my speech, tweaking some of the bits I had planned to do between speakers. I really threw myself into doing a good job, and I did. I was the highlight of the wedding.

Everyone said that I killed.

Dominus Vobiscum

After the disastrous Papacy of Benedict XVI, all the secret societies decided to go a different way with the new pontiff.

The Freemasons were keen to start putting their new genetic engineering technology to use, and so create some kind of freakish monstrosity that would be a continued impediment to population control. They were shouted down by the Illuminati, who were excited about the possibilities of having the first artificial pope.

The Priory of Scion and the Jesuits were in agreement a change was in order, but they could not agree on doctrinal issues (though the Jesuits had half a candidate in mind); the Vril Society was totally useless, proposing it was now time to introduce their alien masters to the world in the form of a scaly lizard-like beast called Todd.

The Creeping Dread Society felt it was time for some sort of cephalopod to hold the office, and the Skull and Bones felt that this was Jeb's time.

In the end, they opted for a mixture of approaches — with considerable help from Sony — and the first RoboPope was introduced to the world.

Career Day for Jim

School was lame. Adults were lame. Life, itself, was a series of lame events. None more so than Career Day.

These were Jim's thoughts as he walked into the gymnasium of Beaverbrook High. At least he didn't have to sit through the tedium and ennui of Mr. Leekie's calculus class, or the thinly-veiled severe depression of Ms. Bentz, his English Composition teacher.

All that dark poetry....

Jim shrugged the painfully lame recitations of Ms. Bentz's poetry aside, and checked out this year's Cavalcade of Losers. These were the employers, the good corporate "citizens" of his home town with suggestions on how its young adults could plan for an exciting life serving hamburgers.

At least he wasn't in class.

He had to admit, the selection was good this year, if pointless. There were some lawyers, some engineers from the city, and a large crowd of kids was milling around the booth hosted by a company in town that made web games. *As if*, Jim thought.

He sighed. This was his last year in high school and he still didn't know what he wanted to do. His marks were good enough for university, but he knew his family couldn't afford it — and the thought of taking all that debt was just too much. His family was on the verge of losing their house. He wasn't supposed to know that, but he did. It was hyper-lame.

Then he heard a voice behind him: "Arrr, Jim. Have ye considered a life at sea?"

pirate therapy ○ 151

About the Author

Simian-obsessed, massively-bestselling-robot-fighting-pirate wannabe, Mark A. Rayner is a writer of satirical and speculative fiction. He is the author of two novels, dozens of short stories, several plays, innumerable squibs and other drivel. (Some pure, and some quite tainted with meaning.) By day, Mark teaches his bemused students at the Faculty of Information and Media Studies (at The University of Western Ontario) how to construct digital images, web sites, and viable information architectures that will not become self-aware and destroy all humans.

He is not a pirate, but he has played one on the stage.

You can track Mark online at his website, where the offer of cake is purely *pro forma*:

markarayner.com

Many of the flash fictions from this collection have been culled from his regular blog, The Skwib, which you can find at:

skwib.com

Links and artwork for many of the pieces in this collection are available at:

piratetherapy.ca

Acknowledgments

Many thanks to the people who helped with preparing this manuscript. Please do not hold them responsible for the emotional or aesthetic trauma you may have suffered. To the other members of the Emily Chesley Reading Circle, in particular, I say: "Damn the Norwegians," particularly Dave Lurie, who is a nit-picker extraordinaire, and a literary life-saver. Substantial proofing help was provided by The Dude, John Anderson, Heather McDonald and Susan Weekes. Cover design by the incomparable The Head of State. I must credit Tobias Lunchbreath for the concept of "laser beans" and encourage you to see his illustration of it. (Available on the book website.) Author photo by David Redding. Thanks also, to the various publications who have deigned to print and digitize some of this nonsense previously:

"Jesussic Park" (*Hobo Pancakes*, August, 2011)
"Disquieting Postcards I've Recently Received from My Future Self" (*AE – The Canadian Science Fiction Review*, Vol. 1, 1, 2011)
"An outraged diner emails the In-Vitro Café" (*Defenestration Magazine*, Fall Issue, 2010)
"Restraint" (*When Falls the Coliseum*, March 2010)
"The Five Second Rule"& "Apocalypse Cow", *Name Your Tale*, 2010
"Rebranding Thor" (*Defenestration Magazine - Literary Humor*, April Issue 2009)
"The Epiphany of Leonard's Toenails" (*Yareah Magazine*, April 2009)
"A Reluctant Emcee" (*Abyss & Apex*, Oct. 2004)
"The Monkey's Tail, as Told by Marcel Duchamp the Day After Charles Lindbergh Landed at Le Bourget Field" (*Trunk Stories*, Issue #2, December 2004)
"The rush of heaven downward" (*Flash Me*, October 2003)

The Amadeus Net

by Mark A. Rayner

Wolfgang Amadeus Mozart walks into the sex change clinic, determined to have his "sprouter" snipped off. So begins *The Amadeus Net*, a satirical novel that explores art, love, and identity at the end of the world.

The year is 2028. For more than two centuries, the one-time wunderkind has kept his existence secret while he tried to understand his immortality. Living in style through funds raised by selling "lost" Mozart works, he has also helped to create Ipolis, a utopian city-state, after the cataclysmic Shudder, a global disaster caused by an asteroid strike in 2015.

But a few complications mar Mozart's perfect world.

The woman he loves is a lesbian, which, paradoxically, makes him forget about his sex-change plans. The world's greatest reporter knows he's still alive and will stop at nothing to expose him. The stakes are higher than he knows, because if the reporter finds him, so will the spy planning to sell Mozart's DNA to the highest bidder. Oh, and, by the way, the world might end in seven days.

Mozart's only allies are a psychotic American artist, a bland Canadian diplomat, and the city itself: a sapient, thinking machine that screws up as only a sapient, thinking machine can.

More info at: theamadeusnet.ca

Selected Reviews

A comic dance in a post-apocalyptic utopia.
~*Book Blog*

Rayner's flair for sustained humor, and compelling storytelling enhances the preposterous premises ...
~ *Flash Me Magazine*

... pokes fun at a variety of modern trends and foibles, and ... does so wittily and entertainingly.
~Donald D'Ammassa, Author of *Narcissus*

At a time when the bestseller lists are dominated by the continuous, unenthusiastic, and barely literate conspiracy ramblings of a *Hardy Boys* wannabe, a story that makes you think and laugh is almost a hidden treasure. To close on the hopeful words of Mozart himself, 'Everyone laugh! Fart, and laugh! Then compose something beautiful.'
~Corey Redekop, Author of *Shelf Monkey*

The story is simultaneously light, deep, silly and poignant. In the hands of a lesser author, an attempt like this could very well become a dispassionate dog's breakfast. But in Rayner's deft hands and mind, it leads the reader deep into the city in which the story takes place (and the city itself is actually a character in its own right!), and into the minds, hearts and souls of the characters. It seems a great many novels I read aren't able to focus on creating more than a couple of full, rich characters, surrounded by a somewhat superficial group of cardboard plot devices. Not so with *Amadeus* and there within, I believe, lies its greatest strength.
~Calvin Chayce, on *Goodreads*

Marvellous Hairy

-a novel in five fractals-

by Mark A. Rayner

So hair is sprouting in unspeakable places and you can no longer carry a tune, but if you're a surrealistic artiste with an addiction to Freudian mythology and guilt-free sex, turning into a monkey has its upsides.

Nick Motbot may be evolving as a novelist, but his friends aren't too sure about his DNA. At least, not since Gargantuan Enterprises started experimenting with it. Once they figure out what's happening to him, they decide to set things right.

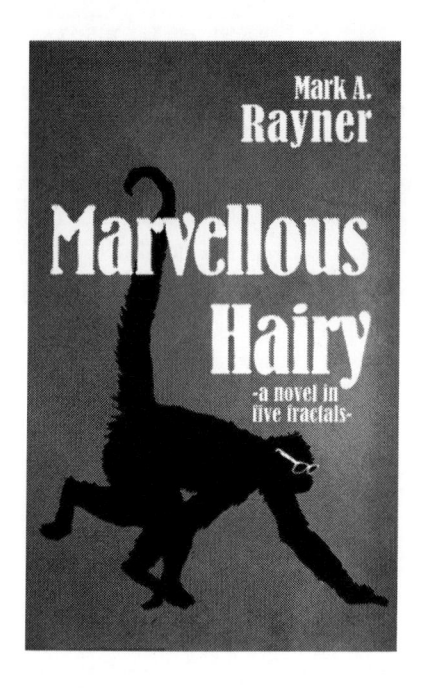

Marvellous Hairy is a satirical novel about a group of friends sticking it to *the man* the only way they know how, with equal parts grain alcohol and applied Chaos Theory.

Part literary fun-ride and part slapstick comedy, *Marvellous Hairy* is about the power of friendship and love, technology run amok, and the dangers of letting corrupt CEOs run our world. But most importantly, it's about how we have to get in touch with our fun-loving inner monkeys.

More information at: marvelloushairy.ca

Selected Reviews

Marvellous Hairy is a top pick for any humorous fiction collection, highly recommended."
> ~*Midwest Book Review*

Mark A. Rayner is an author with a fantastical sense of humor and a dangerous imagination.
> ~*The Next Best Book Club*

Marvellous Hairy is a weird little beast, a blending of the anything-for-a-laugh mentality of Douglas Adams with the experimental abandon of early Philip K. Dick.
> ~Corey Redekop, author of *Shelf Monkey*

Rayner's prose is succinct and exudes humor and wit that only comes with real talent and careful planning—he isn't just throwing a bunch of one-liners on the page, each sentence has meaning and purpose; and the fact that he gets a laugh for it is just a bonus.
> ~*Book Fetish*

Marvellous Hairy is a funny, engaging novel about serious issues but it is never in danger of becoming didactic or angry – Rayner manages to walk this line with skill and with, I would imagine, a smile on his face.
> ~*Bookscout*

...it is such a bizarre barrel of works that you can't help but have fun reading it.
> ~*Phronk.com*

Printed in Great Britain
by Amazon.co.uk, Ltd.,
Marston Gate.